Prais ... **have left Harpo sp** ... **m Tenn**

Don't miss the bestselling CASTLE books
by John DeChancie:

Our adventures begin at

CASTLE PERILOUS
*. . . where magic and mayhem lurk behind
every door—all 144,000 of them.*

CASTLE FOR RENT
*While the king's stuck in a time warp,
Castle Perilous is overtaken—
by nasty blue demons!*

CASTLE KIDNAPPED
*Can Lord Incarnadine protect the Castle
from magic gone awry?*

CASTLE WAR!
*War is hell—especially when the enemy
is a hostile army of alter egos!*

CASTLE MURDERS
*How do you catch a killer in a castle
with 144,000 back doors?*

CASTLE DREAMS
*Is it lights out for Lord Inky? Or just a temporary
lapse into a strange and wacky world?*

CASTLE SPELLBOUND
*When good spells go bad, it's no time
to panic—it's Party Time!*

Ace Books by John DeChancie

CASTLE PERILOUS
CASTLE FOR RENT
CASTLE KIDNAPPED
CASTLE WAR!
CASTLE MURDERS
CASTLE DREAMS
CASTLE SPELLBOUND
THE KRUTON INTERFACE

The Skyway Trilogy

STARRIGGER
RED LIMIT FREEWAY
PARADOX ALLEY

THE KRUTON INTERFACE

JOHN DeCHANCIE

ACE BOOKS, NEW YORK

This book is an Ace original edition,
and has never been previously published.

THE KRUTON INTERFACE

An Ace Book / published by arrangement with
the author

PRINTING HISTORY
Ace edition / September 1993

ISBN: 0-441-14227-3

ACE®
Ace Books are published by The Berkley Publishing Group,
200 Madison Avenue, New York, NY 10016.
ACE and the "A" design
are trademarks belonging to Charter Communications, Inc.

PRINTED IN THE UNITED STATES OF AMERICA

10 9 8 7 6 5 4 3 2 1

This book is dedicated to the original
crew of the U.S.S. *Repuls(iv)e*

Aleta Akhtar
Barb Carlson
Bill Hohmann
Tom Howell
Nancy Janda
Dave Jordan
Judy Laub
Patrick Place
Gordon Rose

PROLOGUE

The Lord High Judge of Tortfeasors' Court of the Supreme Judiciary of Kruton sat in chambers. Around him were gathered the finest lawyers on the planet Kruton. They were very probably the best lawyers in the universe; for every inhabitant of the planet, from microscopic spoor to full-grown adult slime mold, was either a lawyer or a lawyer-in-training, and Kruton swarmed with billions and billions of inhabitants. Despite this population glut, however, Kruton was united; it was a planetary nation. And it was a nation of lawyers, not of men.

The agenda for this meeting was a discussion of relations between the Affiliated Law Firms of Greater Kruton and various alien species belonging to the Galactic Council of Worlds. Kruton was also a member of that august body.

Specifically, talk gravitated around problems with the race called the humans, whose sphere of influence, the "United Systems," had long been a thorn in Kruton's side (metaphorically speaking, for Kruton bodies did not properly have sides).

"Let's sue the bastards!"

The Lord High Judge of Tortfeasors' Court heaved a liquid sigh and turned his (its) "head," which at the moment looked not unlike a heap of decomposing garbage.

(Krutons could, and regularly did, appear to be different things at different times. A Kruton was a fluid, changeable sort of creature, consummately protean by nature. By human standards Krutons were, in fact, quite disgusting.)

"That, my dear friend and colleague, is the general idea," the Lord High Judge said acerbically. "But the question is, what sort of brief can we bring against the humans?"

The creature to which the admonition had been directed answered: "No, I meant sue them for never giving us a chance to sue them."

"Eh?" The Lord High Judge reflected on this suggestion, his interest piqued. "A tantalizing notion."

"Very progressive," another lawyer agreed.

"Oh, not all that progressive, really," the first Kruton lawyer said. "There've been precedents. One alien race in the Zantac Nebula sued another for being more technologically advanced than it was—and won. The defendant race had never even heard of the plaintiff race, much less done anything to it."

"Brilliant legal strategy," the Lord High Judge said, spreading out viscously all over his bench. Bits of fur sprouted here and there along his body. "Admirable."

"The same legal theorem applies to us Krutons," the lawyer went on. "We're hemmed in by expanding alien species in our part of the galaxy. We need living room. We're running short of resources and we're not good at technology, as every one of our number goes to law school. It's a bad situation. *Somebody's responsible!*"

"Someone must pay!" chimed in another of the best of the seventy-odd billion lawyers of Kruton.

"Well, of course that's true," the Lord High Judge concurred. "The trick is to persuade a jury. However, I do think that particular notion is a bit too radical for the Galactic Court of Interspecies Torts and Claims."

"Possibly," the first lawyer said. "But it's a thought."

"We will take it under advisement," the Lord High Judge pronounced. His body slurried and slid, running this way and that like spilled green porridge. "Meanwhile, let's hit the humans with a big juicy liability case."

"Yes, let's!" the others chorused, shifting and reshaping excitedly. There was much oozing and gurgling and splashing about. For a human, the sight would have caused much distress.

"We need an accident!" said a third lawyer, who was all fangs, teeth, and tusks.

"That would be unethical," the Judge said, sucking three newly sprouted foretentacles.

"What would be unethical?"

"Sthaging an accthident . . . excuse me. Staging an accident. The Law forbids fraud!"

"Oh, of course. I meant, let's set up the preconditions that could lead to a big juicy, potentially lucrative accident."

"Where?"

"Along the Human-Kruton Interface."

"That," the Judge said, "would be an incident, not an accident."

"Your Honor, it should be both an accident *and* an incident. Diplomatic, military, political, the whole schmear."

"I see what you mean," the Lord High Judge said. "Yes, yes. That's the ticket!"

"How can we do it?" asked one prickly, quill-covered lawyer eagerly.

"Well, how about if one of our military vessels, carrying a diplomatic mission, crosses the Interface and, say, runs into an asteroid?"

"Yes, but it would be fraud if the ship deliberately ran into an asteroid."

"Oh. Wait a minute, let me think."

The first lawyer clicked his talons. "I've got it. We'll send the ship out there and have it race around helter-skelter. It's bound to run into some kind of trouble."

"It could start a war!"

"We *don't* want a war!" the Lord High Judge gasped. "We can't win a war!"

"No, a little skirmish is all I'm talking about. Our ship gets blasted. Wait, let's just say it gets heavily damaged. On human territory."

What "faces" there were instantly lit up.

"Negligence!"

"Negligence!"

"Tort!"

"Tort!"

"I like it, I like it," the Lord High Judge said, in his mind picturing himself delivering the final summation to the jury. (After all, he was a lawyer, too.) "I shall speak to the combined chiefs of our military forces."

"Bumbling, incompetent fools," grumbled the fanged lawyer.

"Well, of course," the Judge said. "How much military science can one learn in law school?"

"True, true."

"We must make allowances," the Judge said. "Military prowess is not our forte. Tort is our forte."

The cry went up.

"Tort! Tort!"

"All hail The Law!"

"Hail! Hail!"

"The Law is All, The Law is Eternal!"

A lizardlike creature stood. "Let us bow our fluids in prayer."

All bowed what there was to bow.

"O Great Lawgiver, we petition Thee in this, our billable hour of need . . ."

"Amen! Enough," the Lord High Judge said wearily. "Leave me."

The lawyers all sloshed and skittered and wriggled out of the chamber. The door contracted and silence fell.

The Lord High Judge of Tortfeasors' Court sighed as he collapsed into his natural form, a puddle of green, semicongealed goo that looked like lime gelatin.

"I don't feel myself today," the Lord High Judge complained.

CHAPTER 1

David L. Wanker, captain, United Systems Space Forces, stood at an observation window inside the orbital graving dock and beheld the vast and—to him—obscene bulk of the U.S.S. *Repulse* as it hung in its bottomless repair bay.

There was something in its contours—perhaps in its bulging sensor pods or protruding weapon housings—that made it the concretization of an enormous dirty joke. The *Repulse* was of an odd design: ungainly, ill-proportioned, and almost comically obsolete. Why the Forces had not decommissioned her long ago was anybody's guess, but one thing was certain: recent United Systems defense budget cuts assured that the *Repulse* would continue to be a ship of the line for some time to come. Replacing her was an enormously expensive proposition (to continue the dirty joke metaphor).

Captain Wanker viewed it all with dismay and a sense of foreboding, his freckled pug nose twitching. He looked younger than his thirty-eight years; in fact, his face was still boyish. He had bright blue eyes and a receding chin and practically no beard at all. He was lucky to need a shave once a week. He had always worried about this lack of facial hair.

He considered it a shameful genetic defect.

Speaking of boyish thrills—yes, those forward sensor pods, their apexes stenciled in warning red, did indeed resemble voluptuous breasts. From the distended line of the keel, a huge particle beam accelerator hung like the professional equipment of an old stallion at stud, ready for service. At various places along the hull, orifices gaped and buttocklike features protruded. But the whole effect was more tawdry than erotic.

David Wanker sighed. And now he was captain of this space-going bawdyhouse.

He looked down through the repair bay and saw five hundred kilometers to the surface of the planet below. Epsilon Indi II was a world almost without weather, no clouds to obscure its endless wastelands, which made it the perfect space base. "Ship's liberty" was meaningless here. There was nothing for an able spaceman to do, aside from having an ersatz sexual encounter in one of the base's few simsex pods. The wait for the use of these ran to days, sometimes weeks. Otherwise, there was nowhere to go and nothing to do; no joy houses, no fleshpots, no diversions of any kind. No drunken spacemen ear-lye in the morning.

No cheap thrills, barring one's classification of "mud-humping" as a thrill. He had heard about it. The planet's surface was peculiar. Near the Space Forces base lay great shallow lakes of mud. Bathing in the mud was, according to scuttlebutt, fun and somewhat medicinal—good for a certain few ailments, especially "space crud," a form of psoriasis induced by long exposure to dry, recycled air. There were other mudholes, however, that offered even better recreational opportunities. The mixture in these shallow and completely safe quicksand pits was of such viscosity, texture, and slipperiness as to approximate ... to put it bluntly, the mud sucked; hence, if a spaceman was aroused enough and in a sufficiently advanced state of carnal deprivation (there were simply not enough female personnel to go around, and some of them were—well, never mind), why, he could, trouserless, prostrate himself and let nature take its course.

Not that David Wanker would ever stoop to such a base practice. That was for your common swab. David Wanker was an officer and a gentleman. He had just spent three weeks down there and hadn't gone near the simsex pods, much less the mudholes.

Again he took in the ugliness of the *Repulse*. Its hull bore the scars of micrometeorite impacts and the constant abrasion of the interstellar gas and dust that any starship encounters as it streaks through space at trans-relativistic speeds. The composite material of the hull was scratched and pitted. The repair crew was busy sanding down the worst of it but the task was endless and hopeless. A special detail was hard at work on the prow of the ship, repairing damage done in a recent mishap: a collision with a tanker. Unfortunately, mishaps were not unusual for the *Repulse*.

Wanker turned away from the wide view window and almost bumped into a burly chief warrant officer in a stained work jumper.

The warrant officer, some years Wanker's senior, saluted casually and said, "Pardon me, sir. Can I help you?"

Wanker returned a crisp salute. Then his narrow shoulders slumped forlornly. "Only the Creator of All Things in Her infinite mercy can help me now."

The chief squinted one pale eye. "Sir?"

"I'm the new captain of that"—Wanker gestured vaguely out the window—"sorry-looking tub."

Understanding dawned, and the chief nodded commiseration. "Best of luck to you, sir. She's a jinx, that one is. Never saw a ship that had so many strange things happen to it."

"Oh, like what?"

The chief scratched his graying head. "Well, sir, fer instance. Take the last time she was in here for repairs. Total life-support systems failure. But it wasn't just your garden-variety failure. Somehow—sir, don't ask me how—the ship's waste containment system got hooked up with the air circulation network. Some chowderhead connected two pipes that shouldn't have been connected, and liquefied biomass got into the nitrogen/helium compressors."

Wanker was appalled. "Good gracious."

"That wasn't the worst of it, sir. The compressors kept working and pumped atomized sludge into the air blowers. You wouldn't have believed the mess when the biomass hit the rotoimpellers."

Wanker's gray-green eyes widened in alarm. "No!"

"Yes! Sir. Sludge blowing out every vent in the vessel. Everyone got a brown shower."

Wanker looked suddenly queasy. "The very thought . . ."

The chief shook his graying head. "It wasn't a pretty sight, sir, that I can tell you."

"Nor a pretty smell, I'll wager!"

"No, sir. And then there was the time she collided with Admiral Dickover's flagship in a docking maneuver."

"I remember that. Dickover was fit to be tied."

The chief nodded. "Took months to repair both ships. Then there was the time the engineering crew pulled all the control dampers out of the main dark-matter reactor."

Wanker was stunned. "Why in the Creator's name did they do that?"

"It stalled and they thought they could chernobyl it."

"But that's dangerous!"

"Er, yes, sir. It is."

"What happened?"

"Oh, the reactor went hypercritical and they had to do an explosive decouple and drop the whole reactor pod. Only trouble was, at the time they were in an unstable orbit over an inhabited planet."

"You're joking!"

"Wish I was, sir. The pod entered the atmosphere as the reactor was undergoing a hypercritical blowout." Again the chief shook his head in infinite regret. "It was a mess below."

"I should say so, all that radioactive debris scattered everywhere. What happened?"

"Well, sir, fortunately the reactor impacted in an area of relatively low population density. They managed to evacuate . . . and, well, sir, the upshot was that they had to write off a small continent. Could have been worse."

"Dear heavens. Why didn't I hear about this?"

"Hushed up, sir. I got the story from an ensign on the investigating team. Also, I supervised the installation of the new reactor. Sir, there wasn't an old reactor to take out."

"I'll take your word for it."

"And then there was the time—"

Wanker held up a hand. "Chief, wait, please. I'm nervous enough as it is. Thanks for your . . . help."

"Sorry, sir. By the way, sir, may I ask where your authorization pass is?"

Wanker looked down the front of his threadbare uniform. The plastic badge he had pinned on at the checkpoint was missing. He was about to hazard an explanation when he looked up and found a mug shot of himself dangling in front of his face. The picture was on his authorization badge.

"Looking for this, Captain Wanker?" The chief's eyes twinkled.

"That's *Vahn*-ker."

"Beg your pardon, sir?"

"That's how you pronounce my name. Vahn-ker. It's German."

"Oh. Sorry, sir."

"Never mind." Wanker took the badge. "Thank you. Damned thing must have come undone."

Wanker opened the pin, promptly pricked his thumb, and yelped.

"Damn it all, here we are in the middle of the twenty-second century and they can't find a better way to stick a badge on a man than jabbing a pin through him!"

"Let me help you with that, sir."

With the chief's assistance, Wanker was repinned and properly authorized to be present in the graving dock.

Chastened, Wanker said, "Thank you."

"If there's anything else, sir?"

"That will be all, Chief."

"Yes, sir. And good luck to you, sir."

"I'll bloody well need it," Wanker muttered.

The chief went out through the observation bay's only hatch, leaving David Wanker to take one last look out the window before heading toward the gangway tube. Just then he noticed something.

The name of the ship was painted on a forward section of the hull. Some wag had sloppily interpolated two more letters after the penultimate one.

R E P U L S ⁱᵛ E

"How appropriate," Wanker muttered. "How very appropriate."

He picked up his spacebag. It was as heavy as the sense of impending doom that now settled on him.

Inconsolably glum, he left the observation bay.

Lieutenant (jg) Darvona Roundheels, blonde and pretty but perhaps a tad plump, sat at her communications console, idly blowing on her prosthetic fingernails, which she had just painted a pulsing shade of fluorescent pink. Mandarin fingernails, the wickedly curving sort that came in lengths up to ten centimeters long, were the rage this year but regulations forbade such frippery. Darvona had to content herself with nails only two centimeters long, but she made up for it by painting them a new color every few days, or applying floral decals, or gilding the tips.

She was alone on the bridge. The *Repulse* was all but deserted, manned only by a skeleton crew.

Darvona resented being assigned to duty, though she had to admit that she had screwed up badly during the docking maneuver. She had been daydreaming, and—well, it was an honest mistake. Anyone can make a mistake, she assured herself.

Still, it was rotten to draw duty when ninety percent of the crew had liberty. Not that there was anything to do dirtside, except maybe hang out in the rec room and play games. Or find some new enlisted man to have lots of sex with. Or, better yet, find two or three enlisted men to have lots of sex with. Or . . . even better than that—

Her reverie was interrupted by the whoosh of the bridge's access tube as it dropped an ensign to the deck. It was Ensign Svensen, a navigation systems engineer.

Svensen stepped out from under the end of the transparent tube, gave Darvona a cross between a smirk and a snarl, then strode to his control console.

"Hi, Sven," Darvona called, giving him a fetching smile. Svensen was cute but obviously didn't like women, because she had never fetched him with one of her smiles, not even her best model. "What's new?"

"Word is the new captain will be here today." Sven began punching buttons and flipping switches.

"I hope we have better luck with this one. We don't do well with captains."

"Oh?" Svensen said coolly. "Now, what would make you say that?"

"What would make me say it? We've had no less than three in the last standard year. And they've all—"

"Four."

"Four? Has it been that many? Oh, wait, you must be counting the one that got turned into beef stew when the shuttle got crushed between the ship and the tanker."

"Yes. Captain Moore was his name, I believe."

"Poor Dinty. I don't count him, 'cause he was in command only two days."

"He was captain of this ship. He counts."

"Well, if you insist. Four." Darvona ruminated a moment. "Actually, when you think of it, it's all been a result of bad luck more than anything."

Svensen grunted, then gave a mirthless laugh as he continued to work.

"What's with you?" Darvona wanted to know.

" 'Bad luck.' You must be kidding."

"Well, I really don't think it was our fault. The crew's fault, I mean."

"Aside from the captain that got reduced to puree, we had one suicide, one dismissed in disgrace, and one committed to a psych rehabitat."

"Poor Captain Chang. I really liked her."

"I hear she's doing well in occupational therapy."

"And I *adored* Captain Suomi," Darvona said.

"Mr. Rhodes gave a nice eulogy."

"Yes, it was." Darvona shook her head sadly. "Okay, you're right. I guess we do have our problems. We haven't been doing so great lately."

"That's one hell of an understatement. You don't get the lowest rating in the Space Forces by being anything close to 'great.' And don't forget the countless reprimands we've been slapped with."

"Who can forget?" Darvona wailed. "I haven't had a promotion in years."

"We've all been passed over any number of times, so don't feel singled out."

"Somehow, I do. I always seemed to get blamed!"

"Quit squawking. We've all goofed on one occasion or another. We're all to blame."

"I hope this new captain can help us get back on our feet. By the way, what's his name again?"

"Wanker."

Darvona scowled. "Wanker?"

"You took the communication. Didn't you read it?"

"Guess I did, but it didn't register." Darvona pouted. "Great. Now we have a Wanker for a captain."

Sven shrugged, continuing to snap switches. "He ought to fit right in."

CHAPTER 2

Captain Wanker stepped through the gangway tube, entered an unguarded hatch, and arrived inside the starboard quarterdeck airlock of the U.S.S. *Repulse*.

He shouldn't have been able to do this.

He saluted the United Systems colors. Then he wheeled 360 degrees around, chagrined to find no one in sight.

"Is this damnable tub deserted?"

He walked to the right down a corridor for a short way, retreated, then walked down the corridor to the left, searching.

The ship was a mess, wires hanging like multi-colored vines from ceiling panels, plastic pipe and tubing underfoot. Debris of all sorts lay about. Wanker picked his way gingerly over the cluttered deck, wondering if the ship was at all spaceworthy.

On returning to the airlock, he noticed a small desk at a duty station to the left of the hatch. Something rumpled and soiled—a spacebag full of dirty laundry?—was stuffed underneath it. Wanker stooped to look.

It was a common spaceman, fast asleep.

"Of all the—"

Wanker straightened up and cleared his throat before summoning his best command voice and barking, "All right, you son of a mud-humping—" His voice broke. He coughed and tried again. "You, there! Hey!"

The man snored away.

"Wake up and come out from under there!"

No response.

Wanker looked forlornly about for help. Going to the hatch and shouting "Hello-o-o!" down the corridors got him none.

The captain whined in desperation, "Somebody?"

Returning to the desk and sourly regarding the rumpled form of the napping deckhand, he got an idea.

"Wow, catch the butt on that babe!"

The spaceman jerked awake, cracking his skull against the bottom of the desk.

"Ow!"

"Knew that would get something," Wanker said.

"What babe . . . where—?"

The spaceman, who wore the white sleeve stripe of a second-class spaceman, crawled out and jumped to his feet, then blearily perceived that he was in deep water. "Oh. Uh, good morning, sir."

Captain David Wanker was smiling pleasantly at him. "Good morning!"

The spaceman swallowed hard. "Welcome aboard, sir." He saluted.

Wanker returned the salute. "You don't even know who I am. I could be a part of a Kruton commando team."

The spaceman, a short man with pudgy features,

cast a nervous glance about the airlock. "Uh . . . sir, are you?"

Wanker blinked. "Am I what?"

"Part of a . . . you know."

"Kruton commando team? Well, I could be. Krutons can change shape at will. Spaceman, what's your—? What in blazes are you doing?"

The spaceman had reached into a drawer of the desk and had pulled out a quantum flamer, which he now leveled at Wanker.

"Put that thing down!" Wanker ordered.

The spaceman's resolve vanished instantly. Lowering the gun, he seemed confused. "Is this a drill, sir?"

"No, this is not a drill. I'm the—quit pointing that silly thing at me, you incredible idiot!"

The spaceman lowered his side arm again. "Sir, make up your mind, please!"

"I'm the new captain, you boob! Captain David Wanker, United Systems Space Forces, reporting to take command of this vessel. Now do you understand?"

"Yes, sir. But we didn't expect you till later on today, sir."

"Excuse me for being early! Didn't mean to trouble you"—Wanker eyed his name tab—"Able Spaceman Smithers."

"Oh, no trouble, sir," Smithers said.

"Sorry to interrupt your nap. What the devil to you mean by sleeping on duty? How would you like to be court-martialed?"

"I'm already being court-martialed, sir."

"Oh, you are? What for?"

"Sleeping on duty, sir. But the legal officer says

he'll get me off. I have a sleep disorder, sir."

"You have a sleep disorder?"

"Yes, sir. Sleep apathy."

"Apathy? I'll say you have apathy. You mean sleep apnea, don't you?"

"That's it, sir. Apnea."

"Very well. Where's the officer of the deck?"

"The first officer, Lieutenant Commander Rhodes, is officer of the deck today. There's hardly anyone aboard, sir."

"Where is everybody?"

"Breakfast, sir. It's early."

"No guards on the hatch, no officer of the deck. What the hell's the idea, leaving a military vessel unguarded like this?"

"No idea, sir. It's just that everyone's dirtside and there's no one to stand watch during mealtime. It's only for a half hour at a time, sir."

"During which a Kruton commando brigade could . . . oh, for Pete's sake."

"Don't make a move, Krutie!" Smithers ordered, again brandishing the quantum flamer. "Move one tentacle and I'll blow you to the other side of the galaxy."

"I don't have any tentacles, you numbskull! Listen, didn't you receive a dispatch that I would be reporting?"

"Well, sir . . . yes, sir. But you could still be Krutie."

Wanker considered it. "You know, spaceman, you're absolutely right. One thing, though—Krutie commandos rarely work alone. You're forgetting about my buddies—behind you."

"Huh?" The spaceman whirled, and Wanker leapt.

The sawed-off swab proved tougher than he looked, and more wiry. Wanker couldn't take him down, and ended up riding Smithers's back trying desperately to wrench the gun away. Smithers kept wildly turning about.

"Spaceman, put down that flamer!"

A tall, gangling, towheaded officer with commander's stripes on his sleeve came rushing into the airlock. Seeing him, Smithers quit squirming; whereupon Wanker snatched the quantum pistol and slid off.

Smithers was contrite. "Sorry, Captain. I didn't know you were gay."

"What?"

"I'm not prejudiced, sir, really I'm not."

"You are a strange man, Smithers."

The officer jogged up to Wanker, came to attention, and saluted. "Welcome aboard, sir!"

Wanker returned the salute and shook the officer's proffered hand. "Mr. Rhodes, I presume?"

"Yes, sir. Happy to have you aboard."

"I'm not happy to be aboard."

"Yes, sir. I mean, no, sir. Well, we're still happy, sir."

"I'll bet you're ecstatic. What's the meaning of leaving this ship unguarded? A new captain reporting to his ship must be piped over the side and received with a color guard. What do I get? A swab catching forty winks while anyone could come storming through that hatch."

"Sir, it won't happen again. Sir, it's nice to see you, but you just picked a bad time to come aboard, sir. We're undermanned at the moment, and—"

"Never mind. Ye gods, this is getting off to a great start."

Wanker now noticed how extremely tall and thin Rhodes was, and how gawkish and curiously put together he was. With that country-fried drawl of his (*Suh, it's nahss t'see yuh, but y'picked a bad tahm tuh come aboahd, suh*), he came across as tall hay gone quite to seed.

"Spaceman, see that the captain's bag is stowed in the captain's quarters!"

"Yes, sir, Mr. Rhodes."

Wanker jabbed a finger at Smithers. "No, don't leave that hatch unguarded! Belay that order, spaceman."

Rhodes said, "I'll stay here, Captain. Smithers, take the bag. Sir, if you'll just—"

"Stay where you are, Smithers. Mr. Rhodes, I want a tour of the ship, now, with you at my side. Have Smithers watch my bag until someone can either relieve him or take it to my cabin."

Smithers was annoyed. "Well, jeez, make up your mind, sirs."

"What was that?" Wanker snapped.

"Nothing, sirs. Sir. Captain, sir."

Wanker took off his officer's cap and smoothed his unruly red hair, brushing a pesky cowlick from his forehead. "This is ridiculous. I'll take the damned bag along."

"Please, Captain, leave it here," Rhodes said. "It'll be safe."

"I'm not taking any chances. Been a rash of pilfering in the fleet lately."

"I'll sit on it for you, sir!" Smithers piped.

"You mean you'll sleep on it. You do and I'll have

you spaced, chucked out the airlock buck naked."

"Yes, sir. I won't sleep on it, Captain."

Wanker threw his spacebag at Smithers, who caught it neatly. "Sweet dreams. All right, Mr. Rhodes, if we're all squared away now, give me the Cook's tour of this rust bucket." Wanker sighed. "Don't you just love that kind of manly space talk?"

"Always gives me a thrill, sir. This way, Captain."

CHAPTER 3

"Rusty" was in the cargo hold sweeping up the debris left by some last minute recrating. He didn't like sweeping up, but he wasn't about to complain. Jobs as research assistants were at a premium these days. Budget cuts. It wasn't a high-paying job, as jobs went, but it paid the bills and gave Rusty three meals a day. And there were other benefits that were much better than any salary.

The job had given him a chance to travel. Here he was, aboard a military starship far out in space. They were to rendezvous with another ship, the test ship. Once aboard, "Rusty," "Chicolini," and the Boss would begin a series of test runs that would be the culmination of years of experiment and research.

Six long years of work.

Well, not hard work, but work just the same.

Six years of spending government money. The equipment and supplies they'd bought! Millions spent on antiproton generators and microfusion reactors and endless varieties of technological extravagance.

The parties they'd had! Hundreds of thousands squandered on wine and women and drugs and kicky off-the-shelf brainware . . .

Ooops. Better not go into that. But the Boss was in good with the government. He had many and powerful friends in high places. It was okay to throw a little money around, live high, have a good time, as long as you delivered the goods.

Rusty kept sweeping, working his way between high stacks of plastic crates. The overhead lights were few and far between in this part of the ship, and it was getting dark in these narrow aisles.

He heard a sound behind and turned.

Rusty squinted. What was that? Something moving. He stopped. One of the crew, perhaps.

Rusty began to sweep again, but halted. He looked around. Hell, this was clean enough. He started retracing his steps through the maze of aisles between the high stacks.

Squash, squish.

"What the . . . ?"

Rusty looked at his shoes. He was standing in a puddle of something.

"Hey, who spilled—? Yuck, what is this stuff? Darn it, hope I can find a mop."

Rusty walked through the puddle, made a few turns, and arrived at the cargo bay hatch. He went out into the corridor and flagged down a passing warrant officer.

"Hey, space-guy, know where I can get a mop?"

"Janitorial stuff's right in that compartment."

Rusty followed the pointed finger.

" 'Space-guy,' " the warrant officer muttered, walking away.

Rusty didn't find a mop, but this nifty vacuum scrubber would do fine. He hauled the thing back to the cargo bay.

But he couldn't find the puddle. He searched and searched, threading the maze and becoming more irritated the longer he kept at it. It was gone. Dried up. Or it was just something leaking that flowed away somewhere? In which case, it was the space-guys' problem, not his. He shrugged and lugged the vacuum scrubber back to the hatch.

As he was leaving he happened to glance back and saw Chicolini coming out of the stacks.

"Hey. Were you back there?"

"Huh? Oh, I was looking for you."

Rusty's coworker wasn't in character, but then neither was Rusty.

"You know, I didn't see you when I was . . . never mind. What's up? The Boss?"

Chicolini nodded. "He's getting wild. He's always wired, never goes out of character. You better go up and see what you can do with him."

"What can I do with him?"

"You've been with him longer, you know him better than I do."

"Hey, he's a genius. I'm just a lab tech."

"Get up to the cabin. If he blows the project, the politicians might want to know what we've been spending all the money on. In detail. Get the picture?"

"Got the picture."

"So, leave. And get into character."

"Sure. Always do when I'm around the Boss. He hates reality."

"All humans do."

Rusty chuckled. "You're not human?"

"Forget it," Rusty's coworker said.

"Hey, by the way, when you were back there, did

you step into a puddle of something?"

"Something? What something?"

"Couldn't see what it was. Something wet and sticky."

"Forget about that crap!"

"Hey, it could have been lubrication leaking from one of our crates. What do you mean, forget—"

"I'll take care of it," Chicolini said, taking the vacuum scrubber. "You go look after the Boss."

Rusty shrugged. "Anything you say."

"And remember to get into character."

"I'll switch on before I go in the door."

"All right, just don't forget, you know how touchy he is."

"Sure. See you later."

"See you. Don't worry about the leak. I'll look after it."

"Okay!"

Rusty jogged off down the corridor, his tattered trench coat trailing and flapping.

"I'll take care of it. Yeah, sure."

The one called Chicolini retreated into the shadows of the hold.

CHAPTER 4

" . . . and this is the bridge!"

Wanker picked himself off the deck.

"Never have gotten used to these damned blow tubes. Rotten things." He dusted himself off. Then he took a good look around.

"Good *Lord*."

The bridge was in an even sorrier state than the rest of the ship, littered with half-disassembled components and heterogeneous junk. The usual jungle of hanging wire proliferated, but this particular plastic rain forest was positively tropical. Sections of metal paneling leaned against the bulkheads, and the holes they left exposed a raw chaos of electronic arcana. The various department stations—communications, navigation, and the like—were more or less intact. They were spaced widely apart. The huge plates of armored shielding that would, when battle stations sounded, slide down to further separate and protect each station were stuck halfway. This intensified the sense of cramping and clutter.

The armor-shielding design was an old one. Space warships with up-to-date configurations had no bridge per se, so that one well-placed hit could not "decapitate" a ship's command and control structure. The various command stations were mobile and widely dispersed within the ship.

Lt. Commander Rhodes was embarrassed. "Sir, we're undergoing extensive repairs."

"Commander, you have a penchant for stating the ridiculously obvious. Please continue."

"Uh, yes, sir, Captain Wanker. As I said—"

"That's VAHN-ker."

"Vahnker?

"Yes, it's German."

"Oh. I see. Well, Captain W . . . er, Vah—"

"*Vahn*-ker," Wanker coached his first officer. "*VAHN*-ker. Accent on the penultimate."

"*Vahn*-ker. Yes, sir. As I said, sir, this is . . . well, this is the nerve center . . . well, you know. The brain."

"The bridge of the U.S.S. *Repulse!*" Wanker's awe was akin to that of a man viewing a vast and messy traffic accident. "The diseased brain of the worst-rated ship in Space Fleet. The center of the pathology, as it were."

Rhodes, visibly affronted, was nevertheless at pains to be tactful. "Well, sir, all due respect, but I think your characterization is a bit unfair."

"Unfair?" Wanker took the electronic clipboard that Rhodes carried. "On a ten-point graded scale, this ship scored the following on its last shakedown run: Mechanical Functioning: 4. Overall Efficiency: 2. Combined Personnel Performance Rating: 1.3. Battle Stations Response Time: 1.9. Tactical Maneuvering . . . Shall I go on, Commander?"

"Well, actually, sir . . ."

Wanker read on. "Oh, what's this? Double digits in one category? Wait. Intrafleet Three-Dimensional Checkers Competition."

"Good for morale, Captain."

"Then why does the Overall Morale Profile stand at a heartwarming 0.07? There's more. Battle Readiness Quotient: 0.0006. . . ."

Rhodes said loudly, "No need to go on, sir. Point well taken."

Wanker shoved the clipboard at him. "Then stop dissembling and start assembling the ship's officers. I wish to speak with them."

"Aye-aye, sir. All right, all hands on deck, step lively. Line up, there."

The ship's department chiefs lined up along a narrow gap running through the clutter. They came raggedly to attention.

Wanker looked his crew over and did not like what he saw.

"Motley bunch," he muttered. Even the attractive blonde had a frowzy, fly-blown look about her.

Wanker stepped forward and promptly tripped over a trailing length of plastic ductwork.

Rhodes helped him up. "Watch your step, sir."

"Thank you. Damn, it's messy in here."

Gingerly he stepped up to the first officer, a short burly man, dressed in tartan kilt and sporan, who had an oversize shaggy red head and a scruffy red beard. Noticing the engineering patch on the man's shoulder, Wanker said, "The engineer's a Scotsman. What startling originality."

Commander Rhodes answered, "He's Polish, sir."

"Polish?"

"Yes, Captain. May I present Lieutenant Commander Angus Sadowski, Chief Technical Officer. Here's his personnel file, on the reader, sir." Rhodes handed Wanker the clipboard.

"*Angus* Sadowski? A Polish Scotsman?"

"Mr. Sadowski comes from a planet settled by Poles and Scots, though the Poles are greatly outnumbered. The prevailing language and culture is Scots."

"Very interesting," the captain said. "Tell me, Mr. Sadowski, why does it sometimes seem that every last engineer in the Space Forces is a Scot? In your case a Polish Scot, but a Scot nonetheless."

"Aye, sir, th' thistle's gang ta seed, an' clink her bairns maun need, sir."

Wanker stared blankly at Sadowski, then looked to Rhodes for help. "What did he say?" He swiveled back to Sadowski. "What did you say?"

Sadowski didn't blink. "I said, sir, tha' th' thistle's gang ta seed, an' clink her bairns maun need, sir."

Wanker shook his head. "I have no idea what this man is talking about."

Rhodes said, "He speaks only Scots. The Scots dialect, sir."

Wanker's jaw dropped. He scratched his head. "But why does he speak only Scots? Why not Standard, too?"

" 'Ethno-linguistic self-determination,' sir. It's his right, under Space Forces regulations, to speak and communicate in the language of his culture."

"It all comes back to me. Those new regulations just went into effect, didn't they? I should pay more attention to my junk mail."

"I guess everyone has a right to speak his own language and all that, sir."

"Oh, absolutely! Who am I to speak against ethnic self-determination? But this presents a tiny . . . no, a *wee* problem. I do know some Scots."

"Problem, sir?"

"How the hell are we going to understand him?"

"There are phrase books available, Captain."

"And tapes in the language lab? Never mind. Three cheers for regulations. Wonderful! Well, let's look at his record. Ah, yes. The last ship he served on was the U.S.S. *Intrepid,* which underwent total systems breakdown and spent a year in the graving dock. Well, Mr. Sadowski, can you tell us anything about that?"

Sadowski shook his russet head. "Aye, there's mony a weary airt in th' solar wund, sir, for a' that an' a' that."

Wanker looked to Rhodes for help. "Number One, do you have any idea what this man is jabbering about?"

Rhodes shook his head. "None, sir. I don't speak Scots, I'm afraid."

Wanker said, "Neither do I. In fact, I think I pulled a D in Scots when I was in school." His tone became ironically bright. "Well, we'll just have to muddle through. Oh, what's this? Three disciplinary actions in the last year... 'Intoxicated on duty'... 'Intoxicated on Duty'... and... 'Unconscious on Duty.' Quite an accomplishment, that last. Anything to say for yourself, Mr. Sadowski?"

"Fegs, sir, antimatter's a brawer thing ta mak ye fou than whuskie."

"Isn't that amazing, I just read that in a fortune cookie at lunch. My, oh, my. Well, enough of that."

He moved on to the next officer, a petite woman with overlong brown hair, green eyes, and a pixie face. "Who's this, now?"

Rhodes said, "Our navigator, sir. Diane Warner-Hillary, lieutenant, junior grade."

Wanker smiled. "Diane Warner-Hillary. Nice name. Certainly an improvement over Angus Sadowski, I'll say that much. Let's see. Lieutenant, it says here that you missed your last assigned tour of duty as navigator because you weren't there when the shuttle lifted off. Any explanation?"

Warner-Hillary grinned sheepishly. "I couldn't find the spaceport, sir."

Wanker frowned. "You couldn't find the space-port?"

"I got lost, sir," Warner-Hillary said with a shrug. "When I drive I have this, like, totally bogus sense of direction. I get lost all the time, sir. It's terrible." She giggled nervously.

Wanker's voice boomed, as if announcing to the world at large. "A navigator with a terrible sense of direction." An aside to Rhodes: "Don't you find a certain wistful poetic irony in that?"

Rhodes gave an inward grimace, but nodded dutifully. "Yes, sir."

Wanker turned to Warner-Hillary. "Don't you think a navigator having a bad sense of direction is a trifle, oh, unusual? Not to say impractical."

"Oh, our last captain, Captain Chang, thought it was so funny."

"Oh, he did, did he?"

Warner-Hillary said between giggles, "It was a she, sir. Oh, yes, sir. We had a little running joke about it. We'd get completely lost and she'd go, 'Lieutenant Warner-Hillary?' And I'm like, 'How the hell should I know?' " She burst into elfin laughter.

This was apparently quite funny to the rest of the bridge crew. They could not contain their mirth, much to Wanker's chagrin, which he concealed behind a broad, good-natured smile.

"So, that was your 'little joke'?"

Still tittering but fighting to control it, Warner-Hillary nodded. "Yes, sir."

Wanker smiled through gritted teeth. "Those long light-years must have just *melted* away. Who's next?"

Rhodes said, "Darvona Roundheels. Rank: lieutenant, junior grade. Assignment: communications officer."

Darvona saluted. Wanker automatically began to return it, but before he could follow through, Lieutenant Darvona wrapped him in her arms, gave him one colossal smooch right on the chops, and released him.

Wanker was flustered almost beyond recovery. "Well, that was *decidedly* unmilitary, but I appreciate the sentiment." He straightened his uniform and tried to focus his crossed eyes on the personnel roster.

"You have lipstick on you, sir," Rhodes told him.

"Huh? Oh." Wanker rubbed his face. "Is it all off?"

"Right there, sir. No, other side."

"Here? Okay, thank you. Well—" Wanker exhaled, having regained his composure. "Darvona Roundheels, lovely name. Ah, I see her record is spotless. Not one merit or citation to sully the purity of her total incompetence. How did you land a job on the bridge, Lieutenant? For that matter, how did you make lieutenant?"

"I made an admiral," Darvona said simply.

"I . . . oh." Wanker looked flustered again. "Well, at least you're forthright about it. Let's see . . . Hmmmm. Oops. Disciplinary actions aplenty . . . 'Fraternizing with enlisted personnel' . . . 'Fraternizing with enlisted personnel' . . ." Wanker did a take. His eyebrows arched. "Fraternizing with Space Base 27? Well, Ms. Roundheels, you certainly do have democratic principles, that I'll say for you."

Rhodes interjected, "Captain, Ms. Roundheels comes from a culture with very liberal sexual mores."

"And where is that?" Wanker was eager to know.

Darvona broke in, "Altair Six, sir!"

Rhodes added, "A utopian religious colony."

Wanker nodded. "I see." He risked a guess. "Mennonites?"

"No, sir. The Madonnaites."

"Oh, yes, I've heard of them. Something about worshiping an obscure popular entertainer of the late twentieth century?"

"Well, there are a number of those kinds of sects, sir," Rhodes said. "You have your Lennonites and your Morrison Dancers. Then you have, I believe, the Elvisterians. And then . . . well, there are a few others."

Wanker made a disapproving face. "Strange, don't you think? Worshiping ancient song-and-dance acts. Something odd about that."

"I don't like to put down other people's religious beliefs, sir," Rhodes said with inflated piety.

Wanker shrugged. "Oh, well, of course, don't want to do that. I didn't mean anything by it, Ms. Roundheels."

"No offense taken, sir!"

"Still, I don't think it quite proper to kiss one's commanding officer."

Rhodes said, "Lieutenant Roundheels's people have a fervent religious belief in the universal sharing of free love. The lieutenant is . . . uh, especially pious in this regard."

Wanker glanced over her record. "I can see she's been busy proselytizing."

"Spreading the faith, sir," Darvona offered.

Wanker smiled thinly. "Or, to put it another way, busting bedsprings from Betelgeuse to Beta Crucis Four."

Darvona winced. "All due respect, sir, but I beg to differ with your phrasing."

Wanker went on, "At any rate, none of that explains an efficiency rating of . . . oh, this is priceless. 0.00001. Lieutenant, what do you have to say for yourself?"

Roundheels piped, "Medical problems, sir!"

Rhodes said, "Yes, Captain. The lieutenant suffers from chronic Epstein-Barr disease."

Wanker narrowed one eye, puzzled and suspicious. "Another twentieth-century phenomenon?"

Roundheels said, "But I have the latest mutant strain, sir. It's ten times worse."

"Mutant strain?" Wanker asked, strictly out of morbid curiosity.

"Yes, sir. Not only do you feel tired all the time, you also get fat, lazy, and stupid."

"And you have all the symptoms, poor thing. Well, I must say we're forging into uncharted realms of personnel file, here. Who's up next?"

Rhodes announced: "Name: Sven B. Svensen. Rank: ensign. Assignment: orbital mechanic."

"Svensen. I suppose the problem will correct itself when you move up in rank, but for now . . . forgive me for saying this, Mr. Svensen, but that's a most unfortunate name for an ensign to have."

Svensen said dourly, "It gets worse, sir."

Wanker looked at the roster. "Worse? . . . Ohmigod. Middle name, Benson. I don't believe it."

"My mother's family name, sir. Properly speaking, the two names should be hyphenated."

"Hyphenated? You mean, you're really . . ." Wanker's mouth crinkled dyspeptically. "Ensign Benson-Svensen?"

"I'm afraid so, sir."

Wanker dumped the clipboard on Rhodes and threw up his hands in despair. "This is going to be a disaster! This has to be the worst crew of foul-balls this side of the Lesser Magellanic Cloud!"

Rhodes was quick to say, "Captain, it's not as bad as you think."

"Oh? Just how bad is it?"

"Sir, please give us a chance."

"I'm lost," Wanker said blackly. "I'm doomed. The chief of staff has it in for me. I have enemies in high places. I—" Wanker stopped wringing his hands and tried to pull himself together. "Never mind, never mind."

Rhodes began, "Sir, when we get under way, I think you'll—"

"Who's missing here?" Wanker looked about wildly. "Somebody's missing."

Rhodes said, "Yes, sir. The chief medical officer."

Wanker sneered. "Of course! What ship's complement would be complete without the standard-issue ship's doctor, middle-aged and alcoholic, crusty but benign. Well, what's the guy's name?" He glanced at the clipboard. He shut his eyes. "I can't believe it."

"I guess it is a strange name," Rhodes admitted.

"Seamus O'Gandhi? What's strange about that? You meet Irish Hindus every day."

"Exactly, sir. As you know, during the Great Human Diaspora after the invention of the quantum drive, many planets were populated by vastly dissimilar cultures and ethnic groups."

Wanker looked at Rhodes. "If I know that, why are you telling me?"

"Just by way of explanation, sir."

"Thanks," Wanker said dryly. "Let's see here. Disciplinary actions: 'Intoxicated on duty,' 'Intoxicated on duty,' 'Unconscious on duty' . . . oh, I love that one. And he's not alcoholic at all, is he?"

"Doc O'Gandhi's not an especially heavy drinker."

"No, he's a pill-popper!"

"Yes, sir."

"A drug fiend."

"Sir, we don't like to use that kind of judgmental terminology."

"Heaven forbid. Says here he has an 'occupational disability.' Well, makes sense, he's constantly handing out pills. You know, they used to discharge people from the service for this sort of behavior."

"You can't be discharged for a disability, sir."

"Of course not! Hush my mouth. Never, no, never. Okay, what else have we got here? 'Malpractice' . . ." He snorted. "And . . . what the hell's this?"

"Er, self-explanatory, sir."

This time Wanker did a double take, his eyes wide in disbelief. " 'Clinically dead on duty.' Clinically dead? Ye gods!"

Rhodes said, "He overdoses a lot, sir."

"There's practically nothing left of the man. He has a mechanical heart, a surrogate liver, and one cyborg lung."

"I'm afraid he's due for an overhaul."

"I can't believe this man is on active service!"

"Sir, the Space Forces don't attract a lot of qualified physicians. The pay is relatively low, and, well . . . you know."

"But this is ridiculous. The man is a walking medical catastrophe."

"He has many problems, Captain, that I'll grant you."

"Occupational disability? From the looks of his own medical profile, his blood is a liquid laboratory."

"He takes pills to steady his nerves."

"Yes, but the trouble is he gets so steady he can't move. Where is he, by the way?"

Rhodes said, "I ordered him to report to the bridge a while ago, sir. He should be along any minute."

Wanker snorted. "He's probably so loaded he had to use the freight tube."

Rhodes was about to say something further when he was interrupted by the hiss of the drop tube. Everyone looked toward it.

The load that the tube delivered crumpled to the deck. It was the body of an old man wearing a turban and breechcloth, both dyed kelly-green, along with a standard-issue tunic. His skin looked like cracked parchment. The man's overall hue was medium dark, though it was light enough to be suffused with a sickly grayish-yellow pallor.

"What *is* this man, an Irish Gunga Din?" Wanker asked in utter dismay.

Wanker, Rhodes, and crew stared while the body lay there, motionless.

"Well, I mean really," Wanker said, unsure of what to do. "Shouldn't somebody help this man?"

"Oh, he'll come around," Rhodes says. "Backup systems will kick in any moment."

"Backup systems?"

"The bionic medical systems, sir. In his body."

"Oh. Yes, yes, good. But—" Wanker didn't know what to make of it.

With a sudden ferocity, Dr. Seamus O'Gandhi sat bolt upright. One bloodshot eye swiveled in its socket, taking in the bridge.

Then he said, "Jesus, Mary, and Krishna, I am not feeling very well, by gosh."

Wanker eyed him as if he were a curious species of alien insect. "A wreck of a man." He shook his head. "Oh, the ravages of drug abuse."

Rhodes said sadly, "Drugs are slow poison."

"Yeah, but *he's* in a hurry."

The new captain of the *Repulse* walked over to where his chief medical officer sat on the deck.

"Well, Doc. Why don't you regale us all with one of your witty, crusty bon mots?"

O'Gandhi struggled to reply but succeeded only in mumbling.

Wanker leaned over. "Nothing to say for yourself? No terse witticisms? No spare epigrams, quick retorts . . . eh? What say, Sawbones?"

After an immense effort O'Gandhi blurted, "Oh, my, I am going to be upchucking all over the deck."

Straightening up, Wanker smiled appreciatively. "Worthy of Dr. Johnson."

O'Gandhi's vision finally came into focus. "And who may I be asking are you, my fine fellow, eh?"

"Permit me to introduce myself. I'm Captain David L. Wanker."

"Wonker?"

The captain pronounced it for him.

"It is a fine name, pukka sahib!"

"I'm glad you think so."

O'Gandhi mumbled something as he struggled to his feet. Wanker assisted him.

Wobbling, O'Gandhi approximated a salute. "Chief Medical Officer Seamus O'Gandhi reporting, sir." A liquid smile spread over his face. "Please to be calling me 'Jimmy.'"

Wanker smiled toothily. "Why, sure, *Jimmy!* Jimmy, old friend, old pal, let me ask you a question."

"Anything, my captain of mine! I am yours to command, by gosh!"

"Have anything down in sick bay that'll put me out of my misery, quick?"

"Misery? Well . . . I am having some great pills down there that will knock you on your . . ." O'Gandhi suddenly looked sheepish. "Oops. I am nearly putting my foot in it."

Wanker said, "Oh, I'll bet you have some great pills down there. That is, what you haven't stuffed into your gullet yet. No, I was talking about the harder stuff. The darker drink, as it were. Poison, toxins, dread microorganisms. Something that'll carry me away in a jiffy."

O'Gandhi looked confused. "Well, let me to be thinking about this, now—"

"Never mind."

Wanker strode to the forward section of the bridge. He began to pace.

"Listen up, everyone, I have something to say. Through bureaucratic bungling and the cruelty of a basically malevolent universe I've been handed the rottenest assignment in the Space Forces. This ship is a space-going disaster. But I will be bending every effort to make the best of a bad situation. This shape is either going to ship up . . . er, this ship is going to be shape-ship . . . Ahhh!"

The captain whanged his head against one of the overhanging armor plates.

Sven Svensen helped him to his feet.

"Watch the low overhead when you walk around here, sir."

"Those things are dangerous! Ow."

"Yes, sir. Sorry, sir."

"Not your fault. What the hell was I saying?"

Wanker began to pace again, but halted in front of the large view screen on the bridge's forward bulkhead. It was blank.

"Why isn't this thing on?" he asked.

"Out of order, sir," Rhodes said. "Sadowski is working on it."

"Oh. Useless thing, anyway. As if you can see anything in space. How many centuries has it been since a military vessel relied on visual contact with the enemy?"

"It's been a long time," Rhodes agreed. "You were saying, sir, about shipping or shaping?"

"Hm? Never mind." Wanker resumed pacing, his voice stentorian. "Just let me say this. There are many ways to do things in this man's Space

Forces ... and woman's! ... let's not forget the women! ... Just let me say this ... There are many ways to do things in this man's and woman's Space Forces. There's the right way, the wrong way, the Forces way, and MY way. Now on this ship we are going to do things MY way. Is that understood?"

O'Gandhi croaked, "I am forgetting the cultured plague bacterium from Centauri III! It will be killing you real quick, my captain!"

"Shut up! Now, very soon—in a few hours, perhaps, we will be receiving new orders, and we will set out on our assigned mission. And we will complete our assigned mission! Successfully! Is that understood?"

Rhodes shouted, "Aye-aye, sir!"

Imperiously, Wanker surveyed the rest of his staff officers. "What about the rest of you?"

Came the chorus: *"Aye-aye, sir!"*

Wanker said with sudden despair, "I'm doomed. It's over, my career's over."

He moped to the lift tube.

"Would you like to see your cabin now, sir?" Rhodes asked.

"I'll find it."

"But, sir, I'd be happy to—"

"I want to be alone. Besides, I'll be slashing my wrists."

Rhodes stopped, nonplused. "Slashing your wrists, sir?"

"Yes. Send to the machine shop. Have them make me an old-fashioned straight razor. You know the kind? Long thing, 'bout like that?"

Rhodes said, "Er, yes, sir. Straight razor."

"Tell them to make it of a good-tempered steel. None of that composite stuff. And it has to be sharp enough to cut right to the bone in one slice. Got it, mister?"

"I hope the captain is joking."

"I only wish it were a joking matter," Captain Wanker said dolefully as he positioned himself under the lift tube. He raised his head and stared up into its shadowy heights.

"Up," of course, was an arbitrary term in space, but in this case it approximated reality, for the bridge was deep within the ship, almost at the center of its protective mass. Thus, every direction away from the bridge was "up" and out and through the ship. The ship did not depend on rotation for its artificial gravity; otherwise the bridge would have been "up" and the outer decks "down." In space, no one can hear you scream with confusion.

Rhodes said, "Sir, I haven't even shown you your cabin yet."

"Just tell me where it is."

"A-Deck."

"Officer's cabins are usually on A-Deck, Mr. Rhodes. Where on A-Deck?"

"Aft Fourteen, Number Twenty-eight, sir."

"I'll find it." He looked up the blow tube. "God, I hate these things," Wanker said, then in a louder tone added, "Transport tube, A-Deck, please!" He then touched the oversize red button labeled SUCK. "Positively hate these old things."

"Well, sir, lifts are constantly shifting the center of mass, and back when this ship was designed, they didn't know how to handle that."

"Thanks for the guided tour, Mr. Rhodes. Hate it, getting sucked up like a load of . . . *Uhhhhhh!*"

Rhodes watched as the tube bore the captain upward. When Wanker cleared the overhead, he exhaled and turned toward his fellow officers.

He forced a smile. "Don't worry, y'all. He'll come around."

Everyone groaned.

CHAPTER 5

Captain David Wanker was blown upward, suspended by a strong parastatic field. He felt like a bad dinner rushing back up the esophagus.

The tube vomited him onto A-Deck. He got to his feet.

"One of these days I'll learn to do it right."

He wandered around the almost deserted ship, meeting only one security guard, who directed him to Aft Fourteen, Number Twenty-eight.

He approached the hatch to the captain's cabin.

"Who are you?" the hatch asked.

"The captain of this ship," Wanker said. "Get to know me."

"Prove it."

"Look at my authorization badge, you silly thing."

"I want to see your orders," the hatch said.

"Oh, all right." Wanker searched his jacket pockets, found a microdisk, pulled the thing out, and shoved it into the slot in the hatch.

There came a beep. Then: "Wanker, David Ludwig, Captain, United Systems Space Forces, assigned as commander of the U.S.S. *Repulse*. You may enter."

With a soft whine, the hatch rose in its slot.

"Thank you so much," Wanker said dryly. "I don't believe something actually works on this ship."

"Wanker?" the hatch asked as he went in.

"Vahn-ker. You have a problem with that?"

The hatch apparently had no problem.

The rooms inside were small by ordinary standards but spacious for quarters aboard a starship: two rooms, one with a bunk in it, the other with a settee, a chair, and a desk. The head, complete with shower stall, was off the bedroom. There were shelves, clean towels, and other amenities, but Wanker was too depressed to notice. He sank into the lumpy settee and heaved a great gray sigh of despair.

The communications panel on the desk buzzed.

"Oh, crap."

He cranked himself upward. At the desk he flipped a switch.

"Wanker here."

"Captain? This is Darvona. All comfy in there?"

"Huh? Oh, yes, yes. What is it, Ms. Roundheels?"

"A call for you, sir, coming in by cosmophone transmission."

"Who is it?"

"Your parents, sir."

"Oh. Put the call through."

"Aye-aye, sir."

Still dejected, Wanker sat at the desk and looked at the screen above it, waiting. Presently the screen lit up with the face of his mother, Tess Tosterona-Wanker, herself a retired chief petty officer in the Forces. The camera widened the shot to include his father, Frank Wanker, who sat on the sofa by his wife, doing a cross-stitch. David knew the couple were vacationing on a wilderness resort planet named Grenada. Tall purplish trees swayed in the background.

"Hello, Mother," David said. "Hello, Father. How are things at Camp Grenada?"

"Great," Tess told him. "Well, kid, how was your first day aboard the new tub?" As always, her hair was clipped short and flattened on top. Recently, though, she had let her mustache flair out into scooter handlebars. ("Strictly nonregulation," she liked to quip, "but they're somethin' to grab besides my ears.")

"Just reported, Mom. The day's just begun in this time zone."

"Hello, David dear," his father said. "Hope you're eating right and watching your weight. That space chow tends to be so fattening."

David patted his soft, nascent potbelly. "I'm watching my weight, Dad, don't worry."

"Don't worry about what you eat, kid," Tess said, "get exercise. Don't sit on your butt and brood. Get to the gym regularly and work out. With weights, like I do." Tess raised her right arm and flexed her impressive biceps.

"Great definition, Mom," David said.

"Thanks. You were always a pudgy kid. But I tried to bring you up proper."

"You did, Mom. You did."

"Betchur sweet ass, kiddo," Tess said, then upended a beer bottle into her mouth.

Frank asked, "Is your cabin nice aboard the . . . what's the name of the ship again?"

"*Repulse*. Here, I'm panning the camera around the place."

"Oh, that's very nice. The bed looks awfully narrow, though. You were always such a bad sleeper, tossing and turning all night. You flopped all over your bed."

Tess belched, then snickered. "When he wasn't pissin' all over it."

"Aw, Mom, come on!" David's ears turned a burning magenta.

"Just kiddin', guy," Tess said. "Hey, lighten up."

"Sorry. How's your vacation been so far?"

"Pretty boring," Tess said. "Bunch of old farts sitting around playing canasta, complaining about the weather and the food . . . shee-it. I wanna get out into the bush and shoot me a swamp dragon."

"They're pretty dangerous," David said. "Aren't they?"

"Naw. Biggest they come is a couple ten meters long, five high. Small game."

"Jeez, that sounds pretty big to me."

Tess reached off-camera and brought forth a formidable-looking weapon, a short-barreled proton beamer with an immense scope and other flourishes. "Not with one of these babies."

"Wow. New one, Mom?"

"Picked it up before we left. You get one of those critters in this scope, it's ancient history. We're talking pharaohs and pyramids, kid."

"There's only one problem, Tess, dear. Swamp dragons are on the endangered alien species list."

Tess belched again. She crinkled her pug nose. "Yeah. What a bunch of wimps the locals are. But swampies're fair game if they attack."

"Those poor things keep to themselves. Wouldn't hurt a flea unless they feel threatened."

"How 'bout if I chuck a couple of beer bottles at 'em? Huh?" Tess laughed, displaying crooked yellow teeth. "Stir 'em up a bit. Whaddaya say, kid?"

"That ought to work, Mom. But don't get yourself in trouble."

"Don't worry about me, shortie. I can take care of myself."

"Oh, she can, it's true," Frank said, laughing.

"You said it. Listen, kid, cosmophone rates are eatin' us alive, here, so . . ."

"No problem, Mom. Nice to hear from you."

"Stay loose."

"I'll try."

"And don't take no shit from the brass. Unnerstand what I mean?"

"Aye-aye, Cap'n. Dad, nice to see you again. Hey, let's see the cross-stitch."

Frank held it up. White swans on a lake of baby blue. "I've been doing a little cloisonné lately but it's too tiring. So I switched to this."

"Nice, Dad. You sure you're feeling okay?"

"Oh, aside from an occasional migraine . . . and cramps—"

"Hell, he hasn't been worth a plugged millicredit since he was pregnant with you," Tess said. "One complaint after another. Sheesh."

Frank gave his wife a love tap on the shoulder. "Go on. My saying I had a headache never stopped you, you big brute." Frank giggled.

Tess turned her head and spat off-screen. "Fuckin' A."

Frank shrieked. "She's incorrigible!"

"Uh, I have duties to attend to, folks," David Wanker said hastily. "Nice talking to you. Call again."

"We'll do that," Tess told him.

" 'Bye, Mom. Dad."

"G'bye, dear. Take care!"

"Keep a tight asshole, kid."

The screen faded.

"I don't believe I drew this horrid assignment," Captain Wanker said to the empty room. He wanted to cry. But crying in the captain's cabin was strictly forbidden by regulations. Or should be, he thought.

The panel buzzed again.

"Darn it." Wanker reached. "Wanker here."

"This is Dr. O'Gandhi. Captain, I am finding many poisons down in the infirmary for you. All will be killing you very quickly indeed. Oh, it is a veritable festival of poisons, faith and beggorah."

"Belay that order, Doctor. I'm not ready for it yet. Soon, though, soon."

"I will make you a nice cyanide ricky, sahib, you are only having to say the word."

"Well, I'll have to clear it with the regiment," Wanker said. "Stand by for further orders. Captain out."

"Oh, my, yes."

Wanker shut down the comm panel. "Sheesh."

He shed his space boots and dress coat and sprawled on the bed. There were a hundred things he should be doing, but he felt like doing none of them. Studying the ship's schematics, familiarizing himself with the operational routine, calling staff meetings, writing endless memos: all of this and more was necessary to facilitate a change of command.

He wanted only to run and hide. He hated this ship; he had hated it before ever setting eyes on it, and now his loathing and dread had been compounded in the short time since his arrival. What would he feel like months from now?

Years? A shudder went through him.

Wait a minute, he told himself. Wait just a minute.

He sat up and brooded for a moment. Then he got to his feet and began to pace. "What's wrong with you? You're acting like a scared kid. It isn't as if this is your first command. Sure you've made mistakes in the past. Big mistakes."

He paced and paced.

"Okay, *real* big mistakes. Like the *Hood*. You lost the U.S.S. *Hood*. Okay? Big deal. It wasn't your fault! Okay, okay, so the way you lost it was a little strange. It was stolen! Yeah, so what? The board of inquiry completely exonerated you! Those damned aliens are known throughout the galaxy for stealing starships. It wasn't as if you left the keys in it or anything! Right! Completely exonerated. Completely!"

He began pacing in complex patterns.

"Right, okay. Other mistakes? Plenty. Your first command, the light cruiser. Didn't go exactly as planned, but, hey—nobody's perfect. Okay, so you scored a direct hit on a friendly flagship in the war games! It was a great shot! If it had been an enemy flagship—"

He fell silent but continued to make trails across the deep-pile carpeting.

Presently he resumed lecturing himself: "Okay, forget all that. You're an officer in the United Systems Space Forces! You have a tradition to live up to and *goddamn* that blasted comm panel."

Savagely he yanked a switch on the desk. "What the hell is it?"

"Captain?"

"Yes, yes, what do you want?"

"It's Darvona, sir. Am I . . . am I disturbing you?"

"No! Uh . . . no. Um . . . sorry. What is it, Ms. Roundheels?"

"All the other captains called me Darvona."

"Oh, all right. What is it, Darvona?"

"Captain Chang left a recording for you."

"Chang? Who the hell is he?"

"It's a woman, sir. She was the last captain of the *Repulse*."

"Oh. And you say she left a recording for me?"

"For the next captain."

"I see. Well, play the message."

"It's confidential, sir. You have to authorize playback with your orders."

"Very well." Wanker fetched his microdisk. "Okay, it's in the slot."

"It'll be up in a second, sir."

Wanker sat at the desk. "I have to get control of myself," he muttered. "Think of it as a challenge. A challenge. That's the ticket."

"This is the former captain of the *Repulse* speaking," said a voice from the screen.

Wanker raised his eyes and saw the face of an attractive Oriental woman.

"My name is Naomi Chang, and I have a message for the next captain of this fine military vessel."

Wanker waited, intrigued and puzzled.

The woman's face contorted into a tortured mask. "GET OUT! GET OUT! HIDE! WHATEVER YOU DO, DON'T TRY TO COMMAND THIS SHIP! IT'S

A JINX, IT'S A TRAP, IT'LL KILL YOU! THEY'LL DRIVE YOU CRAZY, THEY'RE ALL NUTS! EVERY ONE OF THEM, LUNATICS! IT'S A SHIP FROM HELL! AIEEEEEEEEEEEE—!"

Wanker lunged for the cut-off switch.

The screen went dark.

"Oh, my God," David Wanker said in a small voice, his freckled face ashen.

CHAPTER 6

Over the next few days, none of the skeleton crew so much as glimpsed the new captain, who spent the time sequestered away, taking his meals alone and admitting no one to his sanctum.

Scuttlebutt didn't know what to make of it. Meanwhile, on the planet below, the rest of the crew—mostly enlisted personnel with a few warrant officers—were getting restless. The base's laundry was overwhelmed, jammed with piles of mud-encrusted uniforms.

Captain Wanker called no executive meetings. He did request numerous computer files: ship's logs, data bases, procedural flowcharts and such like. He also tapped the ship's computer for a flood of other data. This behavior was unremarkable in itself, but coupled with his becoming a virtual recluse, it caused some speculation.

"It's our next assignment," Darvona surmised. "He's already been briefed by Operations. It's something big, I'll bet."

"Fat chance," Sven said dourly as he looked at some instruments close to Darvona's console.

Darvona gave him a haughty look. "Well, how do you know it isn't?"

Sven shrugged. "Dream on. Before you do, though, why don't you find out who's sending out that distress call?"

"Huh? What distress call?"

"The one registering on your console." Sven reached and flipped a switch. A loud beeping sounded. "You had the scanning alert off."

"Oh, that distress call." Darvona squinted at the display. "It's only a third-class call. Nothing really to worry about."

"What ship is it?"

"It's a cruiser, the *Anson MacDonald*. Must be having minor mechanical failure. It's requesting a berth at the graving dock."

"Either that or it's coming to take us away on a mystery tour."

Darvona's pretty blue eyes went wide. "No kidding, do you think . . . ?" She thought about it. "Nahhh. Sven, you're so silly."

Sven's eyes rolled as he continued to take readings.

"Hey, here's another call," Darvona said. "From Command Central, scrambled. For the captain."

David Wanker sat at his work console, exhausted and still stumped after days of research. He had been doing detective work, trying to get to the bottom of the *Repulse*'s jinx, to find out why this ship had so many black marks against it.

It didn't figure. There was nothing mechanically wrong with the ship, at least not fundamentally wrong. Yes, Sadowski was a terrible engineer, but that didn't explain everything. Yes, most of the crew were inveterate screw-ups, but that didn't sufficiently explain the mystery either. The ship's operational procedures were standard—hell, they came out of manuals. Chain of command was standard . . . What, then, was the problem?

A beep from the comm panel interrupted his thoughts.

"What?" he growled.

"Oo, Captain, you scared me. What's the matter?"

"Huh? Oh. Sorry, Ms. Roundheels. Look, if it's another message, I'm not in."

"Okay."

"Okay, what?"

"It's another message, and you're not in."

"Right. Wait a minute. Who is it?"

"Who's what?"

Wanker slapped his forehead. "Who's calling, for Pete's sake?"

"Oh. Uh . . . it's Rear Admiral Dickover."

Wanker sat up. "Holy crap. Lyman Dickover?"

"I'll tell him you're not in."

"No, wait! I'll take the call."

"You're sure?"

"Yes, I'm sure. Do you think I'm going to stiff an admiral?"

"I would," Darvona said peevishly. "Enough of them have stiffed me."

"Never mind. Put the admiral through."

David Wanker cringed inwardly as he sat and waited. Admiral Dickover was not exactly one of his favorite people, and he was certain the feeling was mutual. In fact, he had long suspected that Dickover was gunning for him. Throughout Wanker's career, Dickover had remained just above in rank, hovering like a hawk. And every time Wanker goofed, Dickover swooped, going in for the kill.

The blue-jawed face of Lyman Dickover appeared on the screen. He was a study in blue. His eyes had the deadly luster of gun steel, his Earth-sky-colored uniform and the blue-gray stubble on his shaved bulletlike head complementing the color scheme.

"Good day, Admiral Dickover," Wanker said. "What can I do for you?"

The admiral growled, "You can complete your new assignment without screwing up as you usually do."

"I intend to run a taut ship, sir."

Dickover grunted. "We'll see. By the way, we've finally located the last ship you ran tautly. Found it in a scrap yard in the Orion Nebula, its serial numbers filed off and stripped of just about everything, including the main reactor."

Wanker shifted uncomfortably in his chair. "I'm . . . I'm glad we got it back, sir."

"Worth about a hundred credits as scrap metal," Dickover snorted. "But of course the board of inquiry did clear you."

"I was completely innocent of any negligence!"

"So they said. Well, let's put the past behind us. New orders will be coming to you by messenger."

"Hand-carried? From the base?"

"No. The *Anson MacDonald* is carrying the messenger and is being diverted to your area, using a bogus distress call as a cover. You can infer from that how important this mission is and how highly classified, too."

Wanker stiffened a bit with pride. "Yes, sir! Admiral, I relish an assignment like this."

"Relish it all you want. Just don't end up with egg on your face, Wanker."

"That's Vahn-ker, sir."

"What?"

"Vahn-ker. My name."

"Right, sorry about that."

Captain Wanker was nettled, but could hardly complain. Dickover had known him for years and had *never* learned to pronounce the name correctly. Or refused to (which was more probable).

"I think the ship needs a challenging assignment," Wanker went on.

"That scow needs to be sent to the scrap heap!" Dickover said acidly. "Along with that crew of yours. Screw-ups, every man jack and jill of 'em."

"Er, yes, sir. Sir, I've been meaning to ask about that. How could so many foul-balls end up on the same ship?"

Dickover replied, "In any organization you essentially have two options for dealing with incompetence. You isolate it, or spread it out. I myself favor the second method."

"I see."

"Incompetence is sort of like manure," the admiral said with a sardonic smile. "All together in one clump, it's poison. Spread out and allowed to percolate into things, the stuff might do some good, serving as a cautionary example as you deal with it case by case." Dickover leaned back and folded his arms. "The Department of Personnel, though, favors the former remedy. At least they have up till now. For years they've been funneling all the flakes and foul-ups in the Space Forces into the *Repulse*. The result is the ship's sorry record."

"I see. But, Admiral, why did—?"

"Then Personnel came up with a bright idea,"

Dickover went on, falling into his annoying habit of dominating a conversation. "The idea was to assign a skipper who could whip that tub into shape." The admiral lunged forward and pounded his desk. "A real hard-nosed, ball-busting, give-'em-hell kind of a skipper!"

Wanker swelled. "And that was why I was—?"

"And the upshot of *that* was three ruined officers. Two in the bouncy cubicle and one with a slit gullet!" Dickover dragged his forefinger across his throat and made a horrid sound.

"Oh." Wanker's shoulders slumped.

"And then they threw in the towel and gave you the job. I guess the theory was the blind leading the blind. Or to shift the metaphor a little bit, a manure-processor instead of a ball-buster." Dickover cackled.

"Very witty comment, sir. Clever. Clever."

"Thanks, just kidding. Listen, Wanker—"

"Vahn-ker!"

"Vonker, whatever. Listen up. I—"

"Sir, I don't understand one thing." Wanker thought it was his turn to interrupt.

"Eh? What's that?"

"If this ship is a hopeless case and so am I, why have we been chosen for this supposedly important mission?"

"You'll understand when you open your sealed orders. I can only refer to the orders indirectly even over this secured channel, but suffice it to say that the basic mission of the *Repulse* will be changed. It'll be devoted exclusively to testing."

"Testing?"

Dickover nodded. "New hardware, procedures, weapons systems. That sort of thing."

Wanker was taken aback. "My ship . . . you're going to take it and turn it into a . . . a test bench? A target drone?"

Dickover nodded again. "Yup, that's about the size of it. Have any problem with that?"

"But, sir, the crew . . . how can they—?"

"Forget the crew. When you get your orders, you'll proceed immediately to your assigned destination. Most of your people are dirtside, correct?"

"Yes, sir. Shore leave."

"On Epsilon Indi Four? That's a laugh. Anyway, you'll leave them on the planet."

Wanker couldn't believe it. "L-leave them, sir?"

Dickover put a hand to his ear. "Is there some interference on this channel? Hello, hello?"

Wanker gave a tiny groan. "No interference, sir."

"Good. Yes, I said, leave them. Keep any and all security personnel aboard, but shuttle down any remaining enlisted men and women. They'll all be given new assignments. Keep your department heads. I don't know what good they'll be, but you'll need someone to look after your guests."

"Guests?"

"Yes, you'll be taking on civilian passengers. Well, not really passengers. Uh—you'll see what I mean. Now, do you have all that straight?"

David Wanker couldn't find the words to speak. He merely nodded.

"Good. I'll be back in contact with you when you receive your orders. Dickover out."

The screen went dark.

Captain Wanker sat in silent misery for a long while. Then, his arm leaden, he reached for the comm panel.

"Mr. Rhodes?"

After a pause there came, "Rhodes here, sir."

"Have all officers on board report to the bridge within the hour."

"Yes, sir. Something up?"

"New orders. Did another ship arrive at the dock?"

"Yes, sir. The *Anson MacDonald*. Having technical problems, I believe."

"Don't believe it. There'll be a messenger. Send him or her to my cabin. Also, we'll be taking on civilian passengers eventually. Before that, I will speak to the crew—at 1400 hours, sharp."

"Aye-aye, sir."

"Wanker out."

The captain waited a moment, then spoke. "Dr. O'Gandhi!"

There was a long pause before the doctor's ebullient voice sounded from the speaker. "Captain of mine! How are you feeling?"

"Tired, run-down, nervous."

"Begorrah, I am feeling so very sorry for you."

"I need something," Wanker said dully.

"Oh, yes, and I am having exactly what you need. Little pills that will be making you quite happy, singing songs and feeling, oh, by gosh, so very fine!"

"I want lots of them. I want to feel very, very fine."

"I am giving lots! Sure and I am handing them out like candy."

"Send them to my cabin."

"I will be doing this thing, Captain."

"Hurry. Wanker out."

Down and out, the captain thought.

CHAPTER 7

An orderly delivered Dr. O'Gandhi's nostrums and was dismissed.

The courier from the *Anson MacDonald* arrived shortly after Captain Wanker devoured all the pretty pink, blue, and yellow pills the good doctor had sent him. He washed them down with the glass of purple liquid that came with the tray. The stuff looked like grape juice, and tasted like it, but carried quite a jolt.

"Wow. I needed that."

The active ingredient was probably pure ethyl alcohol, fresh from the ship's medical lab.

"An ethanol purple passion," Wanker remembered. He had gotten blasted on them at an illegal party at the Academy. The binge had cost him fourteen demerits and a close brush with being cashiered out of school.

Maybe, he thought ruefully, it would have been for the best if he had been booted out. So far his military career was spotty to say the least.

Wanker signed for the mail pouch and dismissed the courier. Opening the pouch and removing the microdisk, he considered reading the orders in private first, but thought better of it. He dreaded the contents.

He decided to boot up the orders in front of what was left of his crew.

He put on his full-dress uniform, steeled himself, and left his quarters for the first time in two full standard days.

"We've been waiting for an hour," Darvona complained as she checked her makeup in a compact.

"Do you have something else to do, Ms. Roundheels?" Rhodes asked mordantly. "If not, please remain silent."

Darvona snapped the compact shut. "No need to be nasty, Don."

"Look, let's skip the first-name bit for a while. At least until we get things squared away with the new captain."

"Yes, sir, Mr. Rhodes, sir," Darvona said with arched eyebrows.

"Aw, c'mon, Darvona, cut me a break."

"I'm sorry, Don. Er, Mr. Rhodes. Does this mean I have to sleep alone tonight?"

Rhodes flushed, looking around nervously. "Keep your voice down," he said in an embarrassed half whisper.

With impish delight, Darvona reached around and squeezed his left buttock.

Rhodes turned beet-red and moved away. "Please!" he hissed. "Not on the bridge!"

"So-o-o-rry," Darvona said, still grinning.

Sven Svensen coughed elaborately, then flashed a devilish smile at Darvona.

"You keep quiet," she told him.

Rhodes glanced at the chronometric readout on

his left thumbnail. "Now that you mention it, what the devil is keeping him?"

"He will be along shortly, I am thinking," Dr. O'Gandhi predicted. "And he will be feeling much better."

"Oh?" Rhodes elevated one eyebrow. "You gave him happy pills?"

"Begorrah, I am giving him a great shitload of happy pills."

"Uh-oh."

"Plus a wee bit o' th' grape, by Jesus, Mary, and Krishna."

"Oh, God," Rhodes said. He sighed. "Then again, maybe it will be an improvement over suicidal depression."

"I would really like to know," Sven Svensen said, "why the rest of the enlisted personnel were shuttled planetside. What are we going to do for a crew?"

"Captain's orders," Rhodes said simply. "We have automatic systems that can run this ship."

"A human crew always does it better."

"You can say that again," Darvona agreed.

"Sure, a human crew is best," Mr. Rhodes said. "Except in our case, I'm afraid. In any event, our people will have to make the best of it down there."

Lt. Warner-Hillary said, "Yeah, well, I've been talking to a few of the warrant officers. Things're getting pretty ugly planetside. I mean, there's only so much mud you can hump."

"I'd give anything to be down there with them," Darvona said dreamily.

Warner-Hillary tapped a finger against her data screen. "Report here says that fights are breaking out, even among the enlisted women."

Rhodes shrugged. "Regrettable, but it can't be helped."

Just then, from the drop tube came a hollow thud and a peevish voice that said, "Ouch, dammit."

"What was that?" Rhodes said.

"Th' parastatics've gang agley again," Sadowski said, striding purposefully toward a small hatch that led to an access bay.

"That's the captain!" Sven said.

As Sadowski disappeared inside the access bay, Rhodes went to the mouth of the transparent tube and hollered up, "Captain Wanker?"

"That's Vahn-ker!"

"Sorry, sir. Are you hung up in there?"

Wanker's voice rang hollowly. "No, just thought I'd sit awhile in something that evokes a human colon."

"Oh. You're stuck."

"Oh, no. This environment is very conducive to meditation."

"You don't sound far away, sir. Sadowski has gone to find out what's wrong. Meanwhile, I'll see if I can fiddle with these controls."

With the heel of his hand, Rhodes hit the pad marked BLOW. Air whooshed from the tube.

"How's that, sir?"

"Didn't do anything."

"Oh. Well, let me try the suck option."

The first officer hit the pad labeled SUCK. Air was drawn into the tube.

"Ouch," came the reply up-tube.

"Sucking doesn't work either, sir?"

"No. Tell you what, blow a little more."

Rhodes did. "Negative function, sir. Any ideas?"

"What the hell, give it another suck."

Rhodes tried that again. "Any better, sir?"

"I've moved a little. Try another suck."

"How's that, sir?"

"So-so. Blow me again."

"Aye-aye, sir. Any luck?"

"Not much."

"Sir, which helps more, sucking or blowing?"

"Well, I like sucking a little better."

"Sir, it must be the parastatic generators. There's no parastatic field inside the tube. You're probably hung up at an elbow."

"Oh, is that what this is? Try giving me a blow job again."

"Sir, I think we're just going to have to wait for Sadowski."

"To hell with that kilted Polack. Get me out of this tube!"

"Yes, sir. With respect, sir, I should remind you that Forces regulations specifically proscribe ethnic slurs and intimidation."

"Quit moralizing, you pious idiot. Do something!"

"Yes, sir."

The rest of the bridge complement had gathered at the mouth of the tube.

"Here, let me try sucking him," Darvona said, reaching for the control pads.

"Wait," Rhodes said, fending her off. "Uh, sir, do you want to be sucked or blown?"

"I want out of this plastic intestine! I feel like last night's dinner."

"Certainly, sir. Just hold on."

"Look," Sven said, "that's his foot right up there. See?"

"Oh, right, I see it." Rhodes raised his voice. "Sir, we're going to try to reach you."

"Do something, for God's sake."

With Sven down on all fours, letting his back serve as a platform, Darvona stepped up on him and slithered up into the tube.

"Can you reach him?" asked Rhodes.

"Uhh . . . I can't quite," Darvona said. "Doctor, give me a boost."

"I am only too happy to be obliging."

"Ooo! Doctor, I said a boost, not a goose."

"What a disgrace I am and asking you to excuse me for a silly bumbler."

"That's it, just push up."

"I am pushing, by gosh."

"I still can't . . . Someone boost the doctor."

Warner-Hillary put her bony shoulder to the doctor's posterior and shoved.

"Oh, my, now I am the goosee."

"Sorry, Doc."

"Uhh . . . there! I have his foot!"

The captain said calmly, "Okay, so you have my foot. What now?"

"Uhh . . . uhhhhhh. Whew! Captain, you're stuck."

"Brilliant deduction."

"You're caught on something."

"Yeah, I guess. Wait a minute."

"What is it, Captain?"

"I think . . . I think it's my uniform. Snagged on something. This damned seam is coming loose."

"On your uniform?"

"No, in the tube, you dummy. The cloth caught in this crack, here, whatever. I can't see, it's behind me."

"He's caught on something," Darvona yelled. "Try to suck him off."

They essayed a number of different approaches, but none worked.

"Look, sir, we're going to try an experiment," Rhodes yelled up the tube.

"With me as guinea pig, no doubt."

"Afraid that's about the size of it, sir. I'll hit both controls at once. You'll be blown and sucked, and Darvona will try to pull you off. Does that sound plausible, sir?"

"Sounds delightful. Let's do it."

They did it. While they did it, the air flow abruptly increased. The tube made a sound like the breaking of wind, and with it came the sound of tearing cloth.

"He's coming!" Darvona screamed.

Wanker and Darvona gushed out of the tube. The entire ship's company save for Sadowski ended up in a tangled heap on the deck.

Wanker groaned, "You miserable . . ."

It took some doing to sort everyone out, but eventually everyone recovered and stood up.

"No bones broken," Rhodes said, palpating his ribs. "So far."

"My uniform is ripped," the captain said mildly. "This is my best dress uniform." He didn't seem very upset.

"Sorry, sir. I didn't mean to jerk you off like that. The air whooshed, and—"

"Never mind, Lieutenant, you did your best. Thank you, everyone. That was . . . interesting."

Sadowski came crawling out of the access bay. He got to his feet and swaggered over to his shipmates, his kilt swishing, a bushy smile on his rebearded face.

He sang:

> "*Aberdeen shall be a green*
>   *An' Dundee be dung doon;*
> *But Forfar will be forfar still,*
>   *An' Brechin a braw burgh-toon.*"

All eyes were on him.

He put his fists to his hips and beamed. "A wee brownie i' th' works. I turned 'im out, the divvil."

"What'd he say?" Wanker asked.

"He fixed the parastatic generators, sir," Rhodes supplied.

"Oh. Good job, Sadowski."

"Thank ye, sir!"

Rhodes asked, "Sir, are you feeling any better?"

"Better than what?"

"Uh, better than the way you felt previously."

Wanker smiled crookedly. His eyes were a bit glazed. "Oh, sure, I'm feeling better. In fact I'm practically insensible. What the hell were those pills, Doctor?"

"They are being an assortment of goodies."

Wanker looked the doctor up and down, as if for the first time. "By galaxies, you do look like an Irish Gunga Din."

"I am taking this as a compliment, dear Captain."

"Green turban, nice touch. Oh, well." The captain seemed momentarily confused. "What the hell did I come here for, anyway?"

Rhodes said, "Our new orders, sir."

"Oh. Right."

The captain took his seat at his console. It was a huge panoramic display, busy with screens and readouts and dials and gauges. It was as confusing as hell. He searched for the input drive, finally found it, and plugged in the microdisk.

"I hope I win the pool," Darvona said to Sven.

Wanker inclined his head to Rhodes. "What's this about a pool?"

"Just a little wager among the officers, sir. On what the new mission will be."

"Oh? Sorry I don't have a piece of that. I'd bet on galactic garbage detail. What's the smart money on?"

"Everyone's hoping for seeking out new worlds, sir, and, in general, boldly going where no man has gone before."

"That's long odds. What's even money?"

"Border patrol, sir."

Wanker nodded. "So, the nominations are to boldly go where no man has split an infinitive before . . . border patrol . . . and toxic waste detail. May I have the envelope, please!" Wanker poked a button on the console.

The crew crowded in to get a view of the screen.

"And the winner is . . ." Wanker frowned. " 'You will proceed to Sector Four and conduct tests of the top-secret Proust Drive.' Proust Drive? What the blazes is that?"

"Sounds like a new propulsion system," Rhodes guessed.

Wanker sneered. "Who the hell is Proust?"

"French novelist, sir, twentieth century," Svensen said.

"Proust Drive," Wanker repeated. "Sounds like a collection taken up for poor French novelists. Sector Four . . . hey, isn't that right on the Kruton Interface?"

"That region is mostly empty space," Rhodes said. "No oversize stars, very little dust and gas. Not much gravitational interference. Not a bad place to test a new star drive."

"But would you want to test a new gadget near a hotly contested bit of territory between the United Systems and the Affiliated Law Firms of Greater Kruton?"

"Well, you have a point, sir."

"Sure I do. The Krutons are the most litigious race in the known universe. What if there's an incident? What if—and this is unthinkable—what if we accidentally cross the Interface? Incur into their territory?"

Svensen whistled.

"Major lawsuit," said Ensign Warner-Hillary. "I mean, like, humongous."

"That's putting it mildly," Wanker said. "Those slithering shysters would leap at the chance."

"How much do you think they'd sue for?" Darvona asked.

"Plenty, but not just cash," Rhodes said. "Territory, trading rights . . ."

"It would be, I am thinking, a big smashing Donnybrook of a lawsuit," the doctor said.

"Aye," Sadowski concurred, nodding.

"So why would Command Central take the risk?" the captain asked.

"Must be a radically new drive," Svensen suggested.

"They must think it worth the risk," Rhodes said.

"I know why," the captain said.

"Why?" everyone wanted to know.

"Command Central is populated by pinheads."

"No comment, sir," Rhodes said tactfully.

"Hmm. Says here we're supposed to pick up the inventor of this technological miracle. Matter of fact, he's aboard the *MacDonald*. Ms. Roundheels, signal the *MacDonald* that we are ready to take the civilian party on board."

"I love a party," Darvona said as she flipped switches on her console.

Rhodes looked over the captain's shoulder. "The inventor of the Proust Drive is going to personally conduct the tests?"

"Says so right here." Wanker squinted at the screen. "Dr. Rufus T. Strangefinger."

Rhodes nodded. "I've heard of him, sir. He's a brilliant man."

"He'd better be, to justify a goofy name like that."

Darvona announced, "Civilian party requesting permission to come aboard, sir."

Wanker was lost in thought. "Proust Drive! I suppose it's a faster-than-light drive, but I wonder what kind it could be."

Rhodes said, "Somebody should be down on the quarterdeck to receive them."

"I will greet them, by gosh," the doctor said.

"Make sure they have authorization passes. Uh, Dr. Strangefinger and five assistants, it says here. And lots of equipment. Ms. Roundheels, inform Security."

"Aye, sir!"

"I will be welcoming them to our ship," O'Gandhi

said as he headed toward the blow tube. "Be it ever so humbling."

"Tell Dr. Strangesinger to come directly to the bridge."

Rhodes corrected, "That's Strange*finger*, Captain." He turned to O'Gandhi. "I don't know what we're going to do about the equipment. His people will have to manage."

"I will be telling the man that," the doctor said, hitting SUCK. He shot upward through the tube.

"Proust Drive," the captain was still saying as he shook his head, as if he could not quite manage to get around the peculiarity of it.

Rhodes said, "Dr. Strangefinger's a genius, sir, but he is a bit eccentric. Some of his inventions have failed to realize their potential."

Wanker turned his head. "Oh? What inventions were those?"

"Well, this isn't the first FTL drive he's come up with, sir. There was of course the Quantum Drive, which was based on his early work, the application of relativistic quantum mechanics to electrostatic field theory."

"Well, we know that works. It's what propels this ship. Though that was a hell of a long time ago. What's he been doing since?"

"But he's been trying to devise an improved star drive for years, without much success."

"What's he been fiddling with?"

"Well, there was the Uncertainty Drive, which was an attempt to utilize Heisenberg's Uncertainty Principle."

"It didn't work?"

"That's just the trouble, sir. No one's certain whether it did or not."

"I see."

"Then there was the FTH Drive."

Wanker looked suspicious. "What's 'FTH' stand for?"

" 'Faster Than Hell.' Dr. Strangefinger has a sense of humor, sir."

"Yeah, a genuine comedian."

"I'm afraid he has a penchant for clever names and coinages, continuing an old tradition among physicists. 'Charmed quark' and that sort of thing."

"Charming custom. Okay, so this Faster-Than-Hell gizmo didn't work either?"

"It was a qualified failure, but it led to the development of the FTLCA Drive."

"I hesitate to ask . . ."

" 'Faster Than a Lawyer Chasing an Ambulance.' "

"Glad I didn't ask."

"Which in turn led to the FTCWFUA Drive."

"I couldn't guess."

" 'Faster Than a Cat With a Firecracker Up its Ass.' But that didn't work either."

Wanker looked depressed again. "Can't imagine why."

"There were other projects that were very short-lived."

"Is there anything I can do to prevent you from telling me about them?"

Rhodes was a bit miffed. "I won't if you don't want me to, sir."

Wanker gave in. "Go ahead."

"Well, there was the Used Metal Drive. It was scrapped."

"Oh, no."

"And the Coitus Drive."

"You're not going to tell me—?"

"Research was interrupted."

"He told me."

"And of course the infamous Penis Drive."

Wanker ventured slyly, "Let me guess. It didn't stand up in tests?"

"It could only be operated manually, sir."

"I believe I'm getting the hang of this."

"But his best invention to date was the Rufus Drive. And the one that, up till now, showed the most promise."

"Rufus Drive. That one worked, did it?"

"Well, sir, the Rufus went up, but the overhead was too high."

With a groan Wanker said, "Why did I think I was getting the hang of it?"

"And then there was the Subscription Drive. That one—"

"Enough! Please, enough. Thank you, Mr. Rhodes. That was *vastly* more than I wanted to know about the illustrious Dr. Strangefinger."

At that moment the drop tube whooshed.

"Did somebody call my name?"

CHAPTER 8

Standing on the bounce pad beneath the blow tube was a strange man dressed in formal attire of two centuries ago: dark trousers and tailed coat, white starched shirt and white tie, a white carnation gracing the lapel of the jacket. For all the finery and formality, though, there was a seedy look about him.

He was not a small man, but he stood with his torso slightly forward and his legs bent, and as he moved it was apparent that he maintained this curious posture while walking. His face was comic in itself: a largish beaked nose jutted out between small round spectacles, presiding over a bushy mustache (though there was something odd about it). His hair parted in the middle and flared out into winglike tufts. He brandished a huge cigar that did not appear to be lit. His eyebrows were as thick as hedgerows.

Wanker stood, took one look at this apparition, and groaned again. Thinking that if he ignored the thing it would go away, he barked, "Navigator! Plot a course for the Kruton Interface!"

Warner-Hillary asked, "Where is it?"

Wanker was on the verge of deigning to speak

to the intruder, but was brought up short. "What'd you say?"

"I mean, sir, like . . . where's the Kruton Interface?"

"In Sector Four."

"Uh, that's a big area of the galaxy, sir. Uh, any idea, you know, exactly where?"

"Haven't a clue, honey. What the devil do I know about navigation?"

"Didn't you learn a little bit in the Academy?"

"Huh? Well, I guess I did. But it wasn't . . . matter of fact . . . you know, I think I actually flunked that course." The captain thought it over. "No, I dropped it and got an Incomplete, then I retook it and squeaked by with a . . ." The penny finally dropped. "Wait a minute, what the hell am I saying? Lieutenant, you are the navigator of this ship. You mean to say you don't know how to plot and lay in a course?"

"Well, yes, sir, but I'll have to look on a map."

Wanker whacked the heel of his hand against his temple. "A map! What were the chances? Unbelievable. Is that really how it's done?"

"Oh, you're teasing me, sir. No, sir, you see, it's just that—"

"Lieutenant, this is the twenty-second century. We have amazing devices now called computers. They're vastly more intelligent than we are. If you want to plot a course to a certain destination, all you have to do is tell the computer, and it'll do it for you. Does any of this ring a bell?"

"Sir, if you'll let me explain. It's like this—most of the automatic mapping functions in the navigational software have been glitching like crazy, sir. The one that does the plotting and stuff is, like, totally grunged."

" 'Grunged.' Is that standard Space Forces terminology?"

"Means it's messed up, sir. I'll have to locate the coordinates manually, and that means I'll have to search the maps myself and find out where the Interface is. Sir."

"Sorry to put you to so much trouble."

"Oh, that's okay, Captain. It's my job, after all."

"Big of you."

The strange visitor flicked nonexistent ash off the end of his cigar. "I don't know about a navigator, but if anyone needs a doctor, I'm here. Meanwhile, is there a Wanker in the house?"

Wanker took a dim view of this sentiment. "That's VAHNker."

"That's ridiculous. Anyway, are you the skipper of this tugboat?"

Wanker's shoulders fell. "Unfortunately, that burden is in my hands."

"Well, a burdened hand is worth two in the bush. Speaking of which, I'm pretty bushed myself. I've traveled the length and breadth of this galaxy. The length was fine, but I'm here to tell you that the breadth was pretty bad."

Wanker looked about the bridge. "Did I walk into a night club?"

"You look like you walked into a lamppost."

"Look, Dr. Strangefinger . . . I presume you *are* the illustrious Dr. Rufus T. Strangefinger?"

"Illustrious? That's a laugh. I've worked and I've slaved and look where it's got me. I can't get arrested. Except for last night. They nabbed me for frequenting a house of ill repute. I got off, though; turned out I was on the wrong frequency."

"What does that have to do with anything?" Wanker demanded.

"It will all be made clear in the fullness of time. You say you're the captain of this garbage scow?"

Wanker folded his arms imperiously. "I did."

"Well, *you* ought to be arrested," Dr. Strangefinger said, jabbing the cigar at the captain. "On second thought, you ought to walk the plank. Or walk the dog."

"We don't have a mascot," Rhodes said.

The cigar jabbed at the captain again. "You have him, don't you? Somebody should take better care of him. You know how much a veterinarian charges these days? More than a lawyer. There ought to be a law about that. Have my lawyers call your lawyers. Then they can all call my stockbroker and we'll take a meeting and do lunch."

"See here—"

"Or do a meeting and take our lunch. Or we could all stay home and have a nice home-cooked meal." The stranger's bushy eyebrows went up and down in a suggestive manner.

Wanker was losing patience. "Are you or are you not Dr. Rufus T. Strangefinger?"

"My name is legion. Matter of fact, when I was in the Foreign Legion, I had a number of names. One of them was 'Filthy Pierre.' "

"Are you or aren't you Strangefinger?"

"Suh, ah have been called many things in mah time," the man said in an accent that was a burlesque of Mr. Rhodes'.

"Yes or no?"

"Suh, it simply is not that simply . . . er, simple. Suh."

"YES OR NO?" Wanker exploded.

"Well, since you put it that way—yes."

Wanker exhaled. "Thank you. Now, just what the devil is this thing of yours, this new drive—what the hell was the name again?"

"You're being coy, sir. Coy, very coy." The eyebrows wiggled again.

"Look, Strangefinger, can we dispense with all this foolishness?"

At a brisk pace, Strangefinger began a spot inspection of the bridge, shoulders hunched forward, cigar pointing the way. "I always try to keep dispenses down. Speaking of money, can you lend me a hundred credits till payday?"

"Certainly not."

"Then can you spare a coin for a poor orphan?"

"You're an orphan?

"My father died before his time. The hangman showed up early. Hello, my dear."

"Hello," Darvona said with a smile.

"And you *are* dear to me, very dear."

Strangefinger sat in her lap.

"You're very forward, sir."

"Well, I'll go forward and you go aft, and ne'er the twain shall meet. Except in the wee hours, at the full of the moon, when the wolfbane blooms."

"Huh?"

Strangefinger slid off and dropped to his knees. "Oh, can't you see what I'm trying to say? I *love* you."

Darvona blushed. "Dr. Strangefinger, I—"

"No, don't say it. We're from two different worlds.

Your parents don't approve of me. My dear, I'm afraid we're doomed . . . doomed!"

"No, we're not."

"Sure we are. Got any hemlock?"

"You'd die for me?" Darvona asked.

"Well, I'm willing to get very ill. But beyond that—"

Darvona suddenly shouted, "I LOVE YOU! TAKE ME NOW, NOW!" She dove on him.

They tussled on the deck before Strangefinger got the upper hand and pinned her.

"Boy, did I get a wrong number!" Strangefinger exclaimed.

"You said 'I love you' to the wrong person," Sven Svensen told him. "Here, I'll hold her till she calms down."

"It's all right, I'm a doctor."

"No, I am the doctor!" said O'Gandhi, who had dropped out of the blow tube in the middle of the fracas.

"Doctor, you'll have my complete confidence and none of my money," Strangefinger said as he relinquished control of the supine and semiconscious Darvona.

Strangefinger rose to meet the withering stare of Captain Wanker.

"Dr. Strangefinger, I have a ship to command."

"I'm still waiting for my ship to come in. When it does I'll ship out."

"You wouldn't know a spaceship if one came up and ignored you," Wanker scoffed.

"Au contraire," countered Strangefinger, "I'm an old space hand. I used to cook meals on a freighter that hauled raw chocolate."

Rhodes asked, "You were the cookie?"

Strangefinger's eyebrows wriggled lewdly. "That's right, I was the chocolate ship cookie. And a sweet job it was."

Wanker was horrified. He appealed to everyone on the bridge. "What is *with* this guy?"

Rhodes said, "Sir, I think I can explain . . ."

"Suh, ah protest. Ah protest in the most strenuous terms—"

Wanker clapped his hands over his ears. "Shut up! Shut up! Will everyone please for one minute shut the hell up!"

Strangefinger looked at Rhodes. "What's eating him?"

"Don't know, Doctor."

"Well, whatever it is, he's giving it indigestion."

"QUIET!"

Wanker made a heroic effort to compose himself. "Look, Dr. Strangefinger. We both have jobs to do. Now, about this Proust Drive of yours. What the devil is it?"

"What the hell do you care?" the scientist shot back, then became suddenly conciliatory. "But I'll tell you. It's the invention of the century. It's colossal, it's stupendous. It cost a pile of money."

"How much?"

"Sorry, that's classified."

"Well, how does it work?"

"Sorry, that's also classified. Matter of fact, I ran the ad for a whole week and never got a nibble. I've been trying to unload this turkey for the longest time."

"What's it supposed to do?"

"I'll tell you this, Captain. If it works, you'll be out of a job."

"Thank God! When?"

"Don't be too eager. You'll be walking the streets soon enough. Wait a minute. Didn't I see you walking the streets last night? I know—you were the tall one in the magenta frock."

"Oh, frock off."

"Very funny, Captain, but I'm not going to engage in a battle of wits with you. I'd never attack an unarmed man."

Rhodes broke in, "Doctor, am I to understand that your mechanism is another attempt at supplanting a starship crew with an advanced computer system?"

"We've gone through so many of those," Warner-Hillary said with a trace of bitterness. "They're always trying to eliminate good honest working people."

"And none of those systems has ever worked," Rhodes pointed out.

Strangefinger shook his head. "I'm all for working people. Why, my record on labor issues is a hundred percent for other people working."

"Then this Proust device isn't an attempt at total automation?" Rhodes asked.

"No. It's primarily two things: a radically new interstellar drive, and a cybernetic-bionic approach to starship systems control and command involving resonating positive and negative feedback loops in an environment of neural networking." He bent over and whispered into Warner-Hillary's ear. "Impressive, huh? Come to my cabin at midnight and we'll exchange dirty navigator stories."

The young lieutenant giggled.

Rhodes persisted, "Which means exactly what, Dr. Strangefinger?"

"It means, my tall, gangling friend, that the Proust device will primarily replace two personnel aboard this ship. The captain and the technical officer . . ."

Strangefinger broke off and studied Sadowski, who was standing by his station, calmly observing events.

Strangefinger's aside to the captain was: "Don't look now, but your engineer is wearing a dress."

"It's okay," Wanker said, "he's Polish."

"Well, that's different. I was worried there for a moment. As I was saying, uh, regarding the engineer, the Proust device is a star drive and a complete engineering system. Regarding the captain . . . well, just about anything can replace a captain of a ship. All you need is a peg leg, a parrot, and a pillar of salt."

"What about the radically new star drive?" Rhodes asked.

"Oh, that. Nothing big. Just instantaneous travel to anywhere in the universe."

"Wow!"

"A trifle. That's mostly theory right now, but even as the new drive is configured, we ought to be able to treble this ship's cruising speed."

"Wonderful!" Captain Wanker enthused. "I'm all for it. Please go install your device and leave me alone. You bore me."

Strangefinger took the cigar from his mouth. "Sir, I take umbrage at that remark. But I'm a peaceable man, so it's all water under the umbrage to me."

"Why does he keep doing that?" Wanker demanded of Rhodes.

Strangefinger struck a melodramatic pose. "All right, I'll go! Throw me out like a worn-out shoe— my lawyer and I will shoe you for everything you've got!"

"Do I have to call Security?"

"Go ahead. Call Security. Call Social Security, for all I care. Tell them your check was stolen and you're a widow and need comforting."

"LEAVE THE BRIDGE!"

Dr. O'Gandhi helped the recovered Darvona to her feet.

"Very well," Strangefinger said. "I go to make history." He pointed at Darvona. "Or her story. But first I'd like to freshen up after my long trip."

Wanker ordered, "Mr. Rhodes, escort this gentleman to the guest quarters."

"I'll do it, sir!" Darvona said, still a bit flushed and overexcited.

"Ms. Roundheels, stay at your post."

"Have a heart, Captain," Strangefinger pleaded. "Can't you see she wants to make it up to me? She's a simple woman with simple needs. Her won'ts are few."

"I'm waiting for the right man to come along," Darvona said. "Meanwhile, there's nothing wrong with having some fun with the wrong ones."

"Couldn't have said it better myself." Again, the physicist's eyebrows did their lascivious dance.

"Ms. Roundheels, you will please—" Wanker made a despairing gesture. "Oh, go ahead, what do I give a damn."

Darvona's ample hips swayed as she went to

Strangefinger, who took her hand.

"Where have you been all my life?" the scientist asked. "And when are you going back?"

Darvona turned, let go of his hand, and hip-wiggled away. "Walk this way, Doctor."

"If I could walk that way I wouldn't be a doctor."

When they had mounted the blow tube pad, Darvona hit SUCK and threw her arms around the bespectacled visitor. The tube carried them up together.

Wanker was fretting. "I tell you, Command Central has it in for me. I have enemies, many enemies."

"Isn't that a bit paranoid, sir?" Rhodes asked.

"As a personality style, I'm rather fond of paranoia. It's safer than trust and optimism."

"I don't quite follow, sir."

"No, you wouldn't."

A beeping came from the general vicinity of Darvona's comm console.

Warner-Hillary ran to answer the call. "Cosmophone contact from Command Central, Captain. It's Admiral Lyman Dickover, calling for you, sir."

"Old Trickie Dickie again! He's in on the plot for sure. He's hated me since I stole his girl at Space Academy. Put him on the big screen, Lieutenant."

Wanker turned to face a blank view screen. "Oh, I forgot. Wonderful! Well, the little screen, then."

"Aye-aye, sir."

What appeared on the captain's personal screen looked like a moon, its surface cratered and bleak, but then it rotated on its axis, revealing itself to be the shaved, stubbly cranium of Rear Admiral Lyman Dickover. The admiral's perpetual scowl, like a permanent marking on the lunar surface, was still there. "Wanker? Dickover here."

"Hello again, Admiral."

"I trust you've taken aboard the civilian party we talked about?"

"All aboard, sir."

"Don't say 'All aboard,' for God's sake. It sounds ridiculous."

"Sorry, sir. They've arrived safely."

"Good. I'm also relying on you to extend to them every courtesy and comfort."

"Of course, sir."

"And you'll cooperate with them fully. Understood?"

Wanker answered with reluctance, "Understood, sir."

"Bear this in mind. The successful testing and development of this special project is vital to United Systems defense needs. We must have a technological edge against our enemies. Is that clear, Wanker?"

"Uhh . . . that's Vahn-ker, sir."

"Sorry, but the other way sounds more appropriate. Captain, the best way to accomplish your mission is to turn over your ship to your guests and try to stay out of their way. I trust that is within your capacity."

"Give up my ship? You mean, just hand it over? Sir, really, with respect, I must protest. It goes against the grain of a fighting man—"

"Captain, you'll be fighting court-martial charges of incompetence and dereliction of duty if you foul up this assignment as you did your last two. Do I make myself perfectly clear?"

Wanker nodded sadly. "Yes, sir."

"Then bring back a fully tested and operational device. Don't fuck this one up, Wanker. Dickover out."

The screen went dark, and Warner-Hillary announced, "Transmission ended, sir."

Wanker muttered, "Weasel."

Dickover's voice boomed from the speaker. "I heard that! Add a charge of insubordination to that list of court-martial charges. Dickover out!"

Wanker turned savagely on the navigator. "You said the transmission ended!"

"I couldn't read the little thingee, here, sir."

"Lieutenant, the only 'little thingee' I'm aware of is your microscopic brain. Put yourself on report!"

"Sir, communications isn't my job! I'm only trained as a backup!"

"Nevertheless, you're on report. Life's nasty, isn't it?"

The navigator said sullenly, "It's a bitch."

Warner-Hillary moped back to her station. As she passed behind Wanker she stuck out her tongue at him.

"And then you get court-martialed," Wanker murmured to himself.

The captain tried to calm down, using transcendental biofeedback techniques that he had been taught in the Academy, most of them useful for summoning extra mental strength and stamina during combat. He did alpha-breathing, beta-chanting, and gamma-imaging; he visualized his favorite things, and tried to conjure up the happiest moment of his life. He made an effort to feel better about himself, searching within to find an inner strength that he knew he had. He attuned himself to goal-oriented behaviors that would maximize his options and minimize environmental negativity.

"DOCTOR!"

O'Gandhi came running. "What is it, O my Captain of mine?"

"FOR GOD'S SAKE GIVE ME SOMETHING BEFORE I GO OUT OF MY FREAKING MIND!"

"Here they are, right in my tunic pocket, the happy little beggars."

O'Gandhi gave him a handful of pills, pretty purple, red, and green ones.

Captain Wanker wolfed them down.

CHAPTER 9

Repairs to the ship were just about completed. The chief engineer at the graving dock placed a call to the captain of the *Repulse*, who had once again gone into hiding.

"Sir, we've done just about all we could. But there's just so much that we could do in the way of repairs and refitting . . . well, sir, there'd be no end to it."

"Is this ship spaceworthy?" Wanker wanted to know.

"In a manner of speaking, sir, yes."

" 'In a manner of speaking'?"

"Sir, she'll boost to interplanetary speeds easy enough and she'll hold together. At least I think she will. She'll have no problem going quantum, either, sir, as long as you don't push her."

"What would be our top speed in quantum drive?"

"Q-Level Two."

"Two? But that's barely a crawl."

"Sir, personally I wouldn't chance anything higher."

Wanker grunted. "Very well."

"Sir, the *Repulse* is long overdue for a major, *major* overhaul. In fact, sir, I hate to say this—"

"Then don't. I have to skipper this bucket of bolts."

"You have my sympathy, sir. By the way, nice use of space lingo, there. 'I have to skipper this bucket of bolts.' Nifty."

"Stuff it. Wanker out."

When the engineer's face had gone from the screen he said, "I hate that 'she' business. '*She*'ll have no problem going quantum if you don't push *her*.' Give me a freaking break."

The graving dock crew finished up repairs, such as they were, the next day.

"Take it out, Mr. Rhodes," Wanker ordered.

"Me, sir? Don't you want the honor of taking the ship out of orbit?"

Wanker made a rude noise. "Spare me the honor. Boost the ship out of orbit and make tracks for the Kruton Interface. That is, if Ms. Warner-Whatshername can find the bloody thing."

"Make tracks? Yes, sir."

"And under no circumstances is this ship to attain a transluminal velocity over Q-Level Two."

"Yes, sir. Any further orders, sir?"

"Yes. Leave me alone."

"Sir, are you aware that Dr. Strangefinger and his crew are going to begin their alterations as soon as we get under way?"

"Yes. I don't understand it. How are they going to do that with the ship under power?"

"Well, they say they'll do most of their crucial work when we power down, once we get to Sector Four."

"Still crazy."

"Yes, sir. Dr. Strangefinger's a strange man. But

he has the government and most of the brass behind him."

"Sad, but true," Wanker said. "I've been reading about him in *Midnight People*. What the hell's Marxism?"

"Sir, I don't know. I do know that Dr. Strangefinger is considered by the intellectuals to be some kind of artist as well as a scientist."

"Right," Wanker confirmed. "Says here he's a 'neo-dada existential agit-prop performance artist.' What the devil is that?"

"Can't tell you, sir."

"Seems to me they're just a bunch of artsy-fartsy types who run around dressing up and using personality brainware. 'Wireheads' is the street term."

"Yup. Heard of them, sir."

"But what I can't understand is this fascination for the twentieth century."

"Oh, it's all the rage, sir. Twentieth-century revival. The latest fad in art, literature, science, and that stuff."

"How can you have fads in science? I thought science is above that. What the devil could 'post-ultramod' physics be about?"

"Beats the hell out of me, sir."

Wanker collapsed the screen window holding the magazine text. "Don't know why I waste my time reading that rag."

"It's one of the oldest newsfiles in existence, sir. A respected intellectual journal."

"Can't hold a candle to *The Enquiring New Yorker*. Never mind. I gave you orders, Mr. Rhodes. Carry them out."

"Aye-aye, Skipper!"

"Skipper of what?"

Over the next several days things were quiet in the ship. If Dr. Strangefinger's staff was busy at work making alterations to the ship's propulsion system, no one noticed them much.

The crew did notice the strange sounds coming out of Dr. Strangefinger's tiny cabin. Darvona spent most of her off-duty hours there, but she was enigmatic about it.

"Oh, we're just having fun. Ever hear of a 'happening'?"

Sven shook his head.

"Neither did I. It's fun. Why don't you join us?"

"I'll think about it."

Sven did, and a few hours later he was seen leaving the suite with a strange smile on his face.

"Tell me one thing," a curious Mr. Rhodes asked. "What's the honking all about?"

Sven shrugged. "It's hard to explain."

"And how come every time I pass by, and the door's open a crack, I hear someone say, 'Make that three hard-boiled eggs'?"

"Well, sir . . ."

"Yeah, hard to explain. All right. I guess I'll just have to see for myself what this is all about. You know, just for the sake of ship security."

"Certainly, Mr. Rhodes. It's well within the purview of your duties as first officer."

"Well, sure. In fact . . . why are you smirking, Mr. Svensen?"

"Smirking, sir? Me?"

"Never mind."

"Certainly, sir."

"Thing I really can't figure is how so many people can fit in that cubbyhole."

For the rest of the journey to Sector Four, Mr. Rhodes wore a strange smile. His eyes had a slightly glassy look. All the officers took their off-duty hours in the "Stateroom," as Strangefinger's cabin was now called. Everyone on the ship made the visit at one time or another. And with the *Repulse* being run almost entirely by the automatic systems, everyone on the ship was often in there at one time.

The only other event marking the journey was the death of Dr. O'Gandhi, his third for the month.

"His third?" Wanker said in utter disbelief.

"Oh, it's nothing," Mr. Rhodes said. "He's revived already, good as new."

"Oh, another clinical death?"

"Yes, sir. He really does need some time in the shop."

Everyone hung out in the Stateroom—everyone, that is, but Captain Wanker.

He spent his time watching entertainment, working acrostics, and reading.

"Give me something on the twentieth century," he ordered the ship's librarian.

"Please be more specific," the voice droned.

"Something representative of that century. I want to find out what it's all about."

"It is impossible to designate one artifact or intangible that is representative of an entire century."

"Okay, let's limit it to . . . oh, entertainment. No, art. No, wait, to hell with art. Uh, how about literature?"

After a pause, the librarian said, "What about literature?"

"Give me *the* representative work of literature—play, novel, poem, whatever, of the twentieth century."

"It is impossible—"

"All right! Give me a list. Can you do that?"

"That can be done. Moment."

Wanker's screen filled with a list of titles with names.

"Oh, good."

He read through the list. Both titles and names were unfamiliar to him, except for Marcel Proust.

"Uh, who would you recommend—besides Proust, that is?"

"Any of the works listed are thought by critics and scholars to be exemplars of twentieth century literature. Marcel Proust—"

"To hell with Proust. Who's Ernest Hemingway?"

"Ernest Hemingway was born in Oak Park, Illinois, in the United States of America, Earth, on—"

"Stop, never mind. Who's this George Luis Borges fellow? Forget it. Never heard of any of these people. Maybe I should try the twenty-first century. At least they had Stephen King."

"He was twentieth century."

"Then why isn't he listed here? Shows you how much scholars know. Okay. So, this is it for literature in the twentieth. Right. Ummmmm . . . Okay. Give me something daring. New, innovative. Experimental. Weren't they big on that stuff back then?"

"The work best fitting that description is highlighted."

"James Joyce, huh? Whoever he was. What's the format? Just text, I suppose."

"There are illustrations."

"No video? Hmph. All right, put up the text and . . . You call those illustrations? They're doodles."

"Done by the author."

"Silly. Okay, let's read this thing."

Wanker began to read.

A moment later he sat back with a look of annoyed perplexity.

"What the hell is this supposed to be? What language is this?"

"The author's idiosyncratic dialect of Anglo-Irish."

"Huh? I can't understand a word of it. Is there a translation?"

"No translation is available."

"But this is gibberish!"

The librarian made no comment.

"Take it away. Thank you very much."

Captain Wanker capitulated. He whiled away the rest of the journey in one of the ship's simsex pods.

CHAPTER 10

Lt. Diane Warner-Hillary announced, "Captain, we have entered Galactic Sector Four."

"Begin deceleration to subluminal velocity," the captain ordered. "Continue on present course."

"Aye-aye, Cap'n," said Lt. Commander Angus Sadowski.

The electrogravitic field that surrounded the starship *Repulse* changed polarity. The ship still occupied a bubble in the continuum—an area outside of space and time but not very far from either, in which conventional physical laws could be bent but not broken. But now that bubble was contracting. When the ship dropped below the speed of light, the *Repulse* popped back into normal space and became a conventional physical object again, subject to the usual laws governing its ilk, as opposed to a set of quantum probabilities, which it had been reduced to inside the bubble.

The ship underwent tremendous deceleration in a short time. A partial dispensation from Newtonian physics (as opposed to Einsteinian) was in effect as long as the electrogravitic field still existed. If this had not been so, the ship's occupants would have been squashed to jelly against the forward bulkheads.

The star cruiser's speed dropped dramatically. Slower and slower it went, until the *Repulse* was barely moving at all—a mere hundred kilometers a second. Practically at a dead stop, the ship drifted in a vastness that was more empty than most regions of interstellar space. Here floated a molecule of gas, there a mote of dust. The *Repulse* had not much else for a neighbor, except for a faintly luminescent nebula and an even fainter ring of glowing gas. The latter hung two points off starboard at a distance of about half a light-year.

At last, word came that the captain would come out of his cabin and go to the bridge. Mr. Rhodes and Darvona stood by the hatch, as if in wait of some miraculous coming-out, a white figure in a shroud, perhaps.

The hatch rolled up and Wanker stepped out.

He saw the two standing there.

"What the devil do you want?"

"Nice to see you again, sir!" Mr. Rhodes said. "Just want to accompany you to the bridge."

"Oh?" Wanker grumbled something unintelligible. He looked around. "What's Strangefinger been up to?"

"Not a lot, sir, while we've been under power. But they'll begin in earnest now."

"Crazy business, doing this out in the middle of nowhere."

"Security reasons, sir. The doctor said they couldn't trust the graving dock crew."

"I wouldn't trust Strangefinger any farther than I could spit."

Wanker smoothed his rumpled fatigue uniform, which he'd slept in a few nights. Red stubble grew in tufts on his cheek. He hadn't bathed in quite a while.

"You look fine, sir," Darvona told him, as if reading his doubts.

"Maybe I'd better step into the fogger," Wanker said. "Get freshened up."

"Captain, you're okay," Mr. Rhodes said, afraid that Wanker would never come out again if he ducked back in. "Please, let's go to the bridge."

"Well, all right."

Reluctantly, the captain followed them to the nearest access tube.

The captain seated himself at the captain's console, an extremely complex display of instruments that he had yet to study. He felt guilty about that. Above it hung a huge thing like an oversize helmet—the cyberhelmet, or communications sensorium. It was a virtual reality device that put him in intimate contact with the ship, its environs, its instruments, and with certain key crew members. Used mostly during combat, it was also a tricky thing to master.

He pushed a button and the helmet lowered. He poked his head inside it.

It was dark inside. Was the thing on? It was supposed to be on all the time. Then he noticed a legend in his peripheral vision: TEMPORARILY INOPERATIVE. Well, so much for the cyberhelmet. He pushed the thing off his head.

"Navigator! What is our exact position?"

Warner-Hillary answered, "We're about three

hundred trillion kilometers from the edge of the Kruton Interface . . . give or take, you know, a couple billion kilometers. Sort of. I mean, we're kind of like in the middle of nowhere."

Wanker regarded the navigator in silence for a moment. Then he said patronizingly, "Thanks for sharing that with us, Lieutenant. But can you be a bit more specific?"

"Well, sir, we're kind of like . . . here." Warner-Hillary touched a finger to her screen. "I'll punch it up on your monitor, sir."

"I have it."

"Okay, sir, you see that fuzzy blob there toward the top of the screen?"

Wanker studied his screen. "Fuzzy blob toward the top of the screen . . . you mean the one that's ring-shaped?"

"Ring-shaped?"

"All right, what about it?"

"Okay, we're about three decimeters to the right of it, and a little bit down."

"Three decimeters . . . ? But that's off my screen."

"Huh? It's on my screen, sir . . . Wait a minute. You've got the wrong blob. It's on the other side. The one that looks like a weasel."

"Weasel? Oh, you mean this one? That's no weasel. You mean the camel."

"Sir, it doesn't look like a camel to me. Looks like a weasel."

"Ridiculous. It looks like a camel. See the humps?"

"What bumps, sir?"

"Humps. Those little things there. Little humps."

Warner-Hillary inclined her head. "I can't see any little humps."

"There are two of them, like a camel."

"Sir, it looks like a weasel to me."

"Mr. Rhodes, come here, please."

Rhodes got up from his console and came to the captain's.

Wanker tapped the screen. "Doesn't this look like a camel to you?"

Rhodes studied it. "Sir, that looked like a humped weasel."

"A what?"

"Humped weasel, sir. It's a species found on Proxima Centauri Two. Good eating."

"Nonsense. That's a camel."

"Well, sir, it's backed like a weasel."

"It isn't backed like a weasel, it's backed like a camel."

Darvona peered over their shoulders. "Looks like a whale to me."

Wanker rose from his seat, then both he and the first officer took a step back to regard the screen from a fresh perspective.

"The hell it does," Wanker said.

"Oh, I think it does," Rhodes said. "If you look at it sideways."

"Huh? Oh. Well, maybe."

"In fact, I think it looks very like a whale."

"You're both balmy. Anyway, Navigator, where did you say we are again?"

"Well, sir, just about two decimeters to the right of that weasel blob—"

"I thought you said three decimeters?"

"Well, not exactly three. Maybe two, two and a half."

"The captain's right, it's a camel," Sven said, having gotten up and come to look.

"You see?" Wanker said. "I'm not imagining things."

"Well, it is a bit camellike, sir," Rhodes admitted.

"It's a lot camellike," Wanker insisted.

"I still say it's a whale," Darvona said.

"Oh, come on," Sven said. "That's about as much like a whale as my butt."

"Having never seen your butt, Ensign," Darvona said archly, "I couldn't say."

Svensen guffawed. "Oh, you mean to say there are some butts you don't have an intimate acquaintance with?"

Darvona's eyes flared. "I could say the same for you, you little fruit!" She slapped him.

Sven looked momentarily shocked. Then he became instantly furious. "Slut!" He slapped her back.

It was Darvona's turn for shock. "Catamite!" Another slap.

"Hussy!" And another.

"Buttboy!" And still another.

"What the devil is this?" the captain wanted to know. "An officer does not strike another officer!"

"He started it," Darvona said hotly.

"I want both of you—"

"Sir! Excuse me, Captain?"

"This is a disgrace—What, Navigator?"

"Sir, that was an error."

"What was an error?"

"Our position. We're not where I said."

"Where are we?"

"Okay. See those sounding markers in the middle of the screen?"

"What sounding markers?"

"Those little numbers there, the ones that tell you the density of the interstellar medium in that region? We're right about in there, somewhere."

"Oh, those numbers. Is that what they are?"

"Yeah, it tells you the density of gas and dust and that stuff."

"Okay, what about—?" The captain whirled in his seat. "Will you two stop slapping each other?"

"Hooker!" *Slap!*

"Fairy!" *Slap!*

"Doxy!" *Slap!*

"Faggot!" *Slap!*

"Sir, if you'll just look at the map—"

"Wait just a minute, Navigator!"

Rhodes said, "Lieutenant, please indicate our position by using coordinates."

"That function is, uh, nonfunctional, sir."

"The coordinate-plotter is down?"

"Yes, sir. And I can't get the flashing indicator to work either. But if you'll just go to the right of those sounding markers—I'm sorry, to the left."

"Where, where?" the captain wailed. "For God's sake, where the hell are we?"

"*Flit!*"

"*Whore!*"

"*Pansy!*"

"*Harlot!*"

"Will you two—? Ye gods! Navigator, for God's sake, please, will you tell me, without any equivocation whatsoever, what the position of this ship is in relation to the Kruton Interface?"

Warner-Hillary made a vague gesture. "It's off in that direction."

"Thank you so much. That is truly a big help."

"Well, sir, nothing is really working right."

"We just pulled out of a graving dock after five days of refitting!"

"Sir, the crew was gone during that time, and they didn't come back. The computer tech people are all enlisted personnel, and they're responsible for fixing the ship's computers."

Wanker raised his arms in resignation. "You're right of course, Lieutenant, not your fault. But we really have to know where that verboten territory is."

"Don't worry, sir, we're really nowhere near it."

Wanker looked relieved. "Well, that's comforting." He turned around. "What's happening now?"

Darvona and Sven had stopped exchanging blows and were now embracing, both blubbering apologies.

"They're making up, sir," Rhodes told him.

"How nice. How lovely. All stop!"

Darvona and Sven separated and stared at the captain.

"Sir, what's wrong with a little hugging and kissing?" Darvona asked.

"I meant stop the engines, you twits."

"All electrogravitic thrusters're shet doon," Sadowski said.

"I sleep better at night," Wanker averred, "knowing that the electrogravitic thrusters are shet doon."

"What do we do now, sir?" Rhodes wanted to know.

"Nothing. Absolutely nothing. We hand over the ship to Dr. Whatshisface and stand back. Mr. Rhodes, you have the conn. I'm going to my cabin to surgically excise my liver with a butter knife. I need a little relaxation."

"Have a good time, sir," Darvona said.

"Oh, I will. It's a rusty butter knife."

"Captain," Rhodes put in. "Don't you think you're spending a little too much time in your quarters, sir?"

Wanker glowered at him. "Are you questioning the actions of a superior officer?"

"Frankly, yes, sir. We need you here on the bridge."

"For what? There's nothing to do. I'm going back to my cabin."

As Wanker neared the blow tube, he stopped and asked over his shoulder, "Navigator, you're sure about the Interface being far enough away?"

"Yes, sir. Don't worry about it, sir."

"Good, good." Wanker stepped up onto the bounce pad. "You're absolutely sure now?"

"Absolutely sure, sir. Like I said, we're smack in the middle of nowhere. There's nothing around but vacuum for light-years."

"Fine." Wanker reached for the tube controls.

"Except for that black hole."

Wanker froze. His head moved slightly. "Black hole?"

"Well, there's a singularity marked on the map."

Wanker strode to the navigator's station. "Lieutenant, you said nothing about a black hole."

"Well, sir, it's only marked as a first-class singularity on the map. That covers black holes, cosmic string fragments, and dark-matter vortices. I guess it's never been investigated, sir, so it just got a general classification."

"Where, Lieutenant, where?"

"Here, sir. That little squiggle."

"That's a Greek omega. Does that mean a singularity?"

"Greek omega! That's right, sir. Boy, you're smart. Yes, sir, that's the symbol for a singularity."

"How far away?"

"Oh, a light-year. No, maybe half. Wait a minute." Warner-Hillary punched some buttons and numbers appeared on the screen. "Right, half."

Wanker straightened up. "At our present speed it might as well be on the other side of the galaxy. You had me worried for a minute. However . . ."

Rhodes had come over and was studying the screen. "When they test the drive, we could get a lot closer."

"We won't be driving," Wanker said, walking away. "It's their worry. Actually, I get a wonderfully comforting feeling at the thought of being swallowed up by a singularity. A warm, cozy feeling. Getting all runny inside. Think I'll go see the doctor again."

Wanker mounted the blow tube bounce pad again and put a hand on the SUCK control. He hesitated. "You know, I don't quite fancy going to the infirmary. Think I'll mosey down to the engine room and see what Strangefinger is up to." He nodded. "Yup, think I'll do that. But maybe later. First I have a date with a rusty butter knife."

"Hope everything comes out all right, sir," Sven called.

"Well, thank you, Mr. Svensen. I—" Wanker's smile faded, and he regarded Svensen strangely.

The young ensign's face was completely bereft of guile.

"Something wrong, Captain Wanker?"

Wanker shook his head. He hit SUCK.

Svensen's sly grin bloomed the moment the captain was gone.

CHAPTER 11

The Lord High Judge of Tortfeasors' Court of the Supreme Judiciary of Kruton crouched in his chambers. Today he had spun a web and was waiting for unsuspecting prey to flit into his lair.

His communication device burbled.

"Chief Operative Shlurff of Intelligence to see you, Your Lordship."

The Lord High Judge cackled, then said, "Have the chief operative come in."

The door to His Lordship's chambers retracted, and in rolled a huge ball of fur and claws and talons and tentacles. (Really, the sight would have been horrific beyond endurance to even the most phlegmatic human being.)

The awful thing that was the chief operative rolled into the web and was immediately ensnared. The arms and tentacles and other appendages flailed wildly.

"What's this? Help, help! I'll sue, I'll sue!"

"Oh, you're no fun today," the Lord High Judge jeered. "Very well."

The web collapsed, freeing the chief operative.

The Lord High Judge came out of hiding and flexed his fifteen hairy legs.

"Shall we revert to something innocuous?" the chief operative suggested.

"As you wish," the Judge assented.

Both beings flowed and transformed. The end result was two creatures that resembled jellyfish with tufts of green hair on top.

"You sent for me?" the chief operative asked.

"Yes. I want a complete report of our covert operation."

"Which one?"

"The one concerning the humans."

"There are several."

"The one targeting the Interface."

"Oh, yes. That operation is proceeding apace. It will come to fruition shortly."

"Good. Have you had reports from our agents in the field?"

"We have only one agent involved in that particular operation, and there has been no recent report. The agent is not exactly in a position to file daily updates."

"One wishes for a little more information."

"The more information you have, the less your deniability factor."

"True. But this operation has the potential to yield such a great return that I grow impatient awaiting its outcome."

"As I indicated, the wait won't be long."

"Good, good. Can you give me a definite time frame?"

"You might hear something within one diurnal period."

"Excellent! You're right, of course, in limiting what you tell me to what I need to know. I am satisfied."

"And I'm glad to have pleased you, thus far."

"Yes, there is a beneficial outcome yet to weigh in the balance. But I am optimistic. You have done well, Shlurff."

The chief operative quivered with delight.

His Lordship's communication device blurted.

"Yes?"

"Your take-out order has arrived, Your Lordship."

"Very good, start shoveling it in. Uh, Chief Operative, would you care to have luncheon with me? I am dining in today."

The chief operative almost melted. "I would be honored beyond reason!"

The door to the chamber dilated, and in rushed a flood of putrescent matter, the like of which would gag any coprophage in the known universe. The semiliquid mass was mostly purple, with swirls of yellow and green. It stank horribly.

Very soon, both the Lord High Judge and his guest were inundated to their topmost parts.

"Hope you don't mind trendy food," the Lord High Judge said. "They say it's healthier."

"I love nouvelle cuisine," the chief operative enthused.

"Well, dig in."

Both creatures grew paddlelike excrescences and began to burrow into the floodtide of egregious muck. Very quickly, they disappeared beneath the surface.

CHAPTER 12

Two days passed.

The captain was kept informed of the status of the alterations done to the ship, reports that he ignored. To pass the time, he watched all fifty-seven hours of a cosmophone miniseries based on Marcel Proust's *Remembrance of Things Past*. He did not know it, but the original material had been heavily adapted. In fact, the story line bore little, if any, relation to that of the original French novels. The first cycle of episodes, "Up Swann's Alley," was a sex romp cum action/adventure melodrama in costume featuring chases, flamer battles, and steamy group polymorphous sex scenes.

At first he viewed with passing interest. Soon, though, he got absorbed, and watched the entire series.

At long last, the final credits rolled and the music swelled. He sighed. After switching off the screen over his bed and laying aside all his personal autoerotic gear, he lay back in deep thought.

"Boy, I don't know about French literature, but the twentieth century sure was great!"

In fact, he'd been quite surprised. A question occurred to him, and he thought about it. He failed to find an answer.

"Thing is, though, how do you power a starship with that stuff?"

Captain Wanker decided to visit the power plant control module for the first time since he had assumed command of the *Repulse*. First, though, he decided that he needed to do a stint in the fogger.

Yes, he reeked. He checked a mirror in the tiny head. His beard was in patches. He thought of letting it grow in. No, no use. Maybe it was about time to get hormone treatments and grow a fine crop of whiskers. What the heck, lots of men did it. And women.

But no. He liked being a clean-shaven kind of a guy. He applied depilatory.

He stepped into the fogger stall and turned on the controls. A fine mist began to fill the air and condense against the walls.

Soon, though, the temperature rose and the mist changed to steam, and it scalded him. He whooped and lurched out of the stall, whanging his head in the process.

"Mother fogger!"

He nursed his aching head. Then, carefully, he fiddled with the controls until he thought it safe to rinse off, and reentered. He made a quick job of it and escaped the stall without further injury.

He donned a radiation suit and left his cabin.

Having arrived at the entrance to the control pod, he used his authorization microdisk to let himself through the massive hatch.

"Ye gods."

The place was even more of a mess than the rest of the ship. As this was his first visit to the pod, he had no idea whether this condition was normal or a result of Strangefinger's tinkering. He suspected the latter. Masses of wiring like congealed pasta trailed through the place, and willow trees of wiring drooped from the overhead. Myriad tools lay about, along with bits of uneaten sandwiches and soft drink containers.

"What a sty."

Wanker walked around, shaking his head, his only consolation being that this wasn't his ship any more. He was only the caretaker of this space-going laboratory.

No one was about, as usual. Laboratory? The ship felt more like a graveyard.

A ghost ship.

"Anybody here?" he shouted. Then to himself: "Where the hell is that fraud of a physicist?"

As if on cue, the hatch rose, admitting Strangefinger hand-in-hand with Darvona, who was smoothing her clothing and looking content.

"Can't stay, Doctor. I have duty now. Must go."

The physicist broke wind loudly. "Farting is such sweet sorrow."

"Doctor, you're so witty."

"So true, so true. Well, I suppose I'll have to get back to work sometime."

"When did you start?" Wanker demanded.

"Captain, top o' the morning to you. I trust you rested well?"

"Actually, according to ship time, it's seven in the evening."

"Well, I hope you didn't overeat at dinner. You

can be such a glutton. You should get more fiber in your diet. Try this insulation material with fruit and skim milk." Strangefinger kicked at a shard of foam paneling.

"Thanks for the tip, Strangefinger."

"You two talk nice," Darvona instructed. "Don't fight."

"Yes, Momma," the scientist said.

"Give Momma a kiss. I have to go."

"Can I have a raise in my allowance, Mom?"

Darvona pecked Strangefinger on the cheek before scurrying out of the bay.

Wanker gave the oddly dressed scientist a disparaging scowl. "Dr. Strangefinger, it's against regulations for members of the crew to fraternize with nonhumans."

Strangefinger walked over to him, waving his ever-present cigar. "I highly represent that remark. I'm as human as the next baboon."

"Indeed?"

"Indeed. Besides, I couldn't resist her charms. She's the kind of girl a man could take home to mother. *Her* mother, but what the heck."

"I wouldn't know much about women. I'm no stud."

"Be careful, the walls have ears. And they have studs, too."

"Enough of this pleasant banter," Wanker said. "Are you through installing your Proust Whatsit?"

"What's it to you?"

Strangefinger wandered over to inspect a veritable Gordian knot of wiring that bulged from a cylindrical component.

"Doctor, are you incapable of a straight answer?"

"Not when you ask the question with a crooked tongue. Oh, all right, we have one small item left to install. And the installment payments are killing me."

"Will it work?"

"Will what work?"

"Your gizmo, of course."

"Are you kidding? They call me the Miracle Worker. It's a miracle if anything of mine works." Strangefinger absently kicked the huge cylinder before him. "I wonder what the heck this is for."

Wanker's eyebrows went up. "You don't know?"

"I usually leave the engineering to my staff."

"Come to think of it, I haven't seen hide or hair of your staff yet."

"Not a surprising turn of events for a hermit."

Wanker shuffled his feet. "I'll admit I haven't been getting out much. Anyway, where the devil is your crew?"

"They're making some alterations in the reactor module."

"They're fiddling with the dark-matter reactor?"

"No, they won't go near the reactor. They just need to pound on the control dampers a bit."

"Pound on the . . ." Wanker suppressed a scream. "Ye gods!"

" 'Ye gods.' Wonderful expletive. There's much that's quaint and charming about you, Captain Wanker. Sorry . . . Voinker?"

The captain didn't bother to correct him.

Strangefinger made another stab. "Volker?"

Wanker waved the issue aside. "Forget it. Incidentally, why don't you have your radiation suit on?"

"Oh, a little stray ionizing radiation never hurt anyone."

"So you say. The reactor and the thrusters are only thirty meters from this bay and that's close enough to require all personnel to—"

"I was just about to leave, Captain. The final installation will be on the bridge, anyway."

"Oh, very well. Frankly, I couldn't care less if you want to fry yourself."

"I like to think of myself as a man of taste, but I'm not going to fry myself to find out for sure. If you'll excuse me, Captain Volkswagen. See you on the bridge."

The hatch rose again and Strangefinger stepped out, leaving Wanker to his thoughts.

He wasn't thinking nice thoughts.

Another first for Captain Wanker: a visit to the ship's mess.

"What a freaking mess!"

"That's not very original," the Cookie told him as it served him a Synth-A-Chik sandwich and coffee.

"I mean it, look at this place."

There had obviously been a food fight; several, most likely. The bulkheads blazed with a full spectrum of food colorings.

"Don't think it doesn't break my little cybernetic heart, Captain."

"Did you witness?—of course you did. Well, I'll need your input to make a report." Wanker crinkled his freckled nose. "Hell, why should I file a report? That's Rhodes's job."

"Under the circumstances, Captain, what's the use?"

Wanker turned to regard the cold electronic eyes of the Cookie.

"Oh, and what's that supposed to mean?"

"I mean, sir, all due respect and all that sort of bilge—if this were a *real* ship . . ."

Wanker exhaled a black cloud of discontent. "Rats."

He sat at one of the tables and tried to eat. He bit into the sandwich; he chewed.

He spat his mouthful across the room and turned to glare at the machine designated the "Cookie."

"Don't look at me, Captain, sir. Mr. Sadowski—"

"Shut up, you piece of space jetsam."

"Oh, well, excuse me, sir."

Wanker drummed the table. "This is most annoying."

"No one ever said the universe was a bed of posies. Sir."

Wanker turned his head sharply. "You know what else is annoying?"

"What, sir?"

"The habit of giving a hulk of a machine like a food processor a 'personality' so that spacemen get a warm, homey feeling inside when they're served the swill they're supposed to eat."

"Oops, I guess I went and pushed a few wrong buttons on you, Captain."

"Oh, stuff it."

Wanker left the mess.

CHAPTER 13

Wanker arrived on the bridge to find it in no more disarray than usual. Everyone was there except Strangefinger's elusive technicians.

"Dr. Strangefinger, can't we get this over with now?"

"My sentiments exactly, Captain," Strangefinger said, chewing on his cigar. "The time has come, the Walrus said, to speak of many things. Hey-nonny-nonny and a ha-cha-cha." He executed this last with a little dance.

"Can we proceed with the testing?"

"Sure. Disengage all your control circuits. The Proust device will handle everything."

Wanker began to pace fretfully. Something that had built up inside him over the last week finally burst out. "This is wrong, wrong! A machine can't control a starship! A cold, unfeeling machine can't make the warm, human decisions . . . it can't know right from wrong, fair from unfair . . . it has no sense of justice . . . no sensitivity, no compassion!"

Strangefinger bristled. "Sir, you're making my machine out to be a conservative! I know for a fact that it votes the straight Whig ticket."

Sadowski dropped to the deck and went to his station.

"Very well," Captain Wanker said. "Engineer, turn all control circuits over to Dr. Strangefinger's wonderful invention. I can see this is going to be more of the same monkey business. I'm going back to my cabin and rest."

Strangefinger said with feigned sincerity, "Rest easy, Captain . . . and take my hand in congratulations for a job well done." The scientist extended his hand.

Wanker took it and was nonplused when the hand detached from Strangefinger's arm. It was a cheap prosthesis.

"You idiot." Wanker handed him his hand back.

"You've got to hand it to me, Captain."

"Oh, stuff it. Maybe I won't go to my cabin. I think I'll stay here and see what this business is all about."

"Just stay out of the way," Strangefinger said, screwing his hand back on. "You're redundant now. Superfluous. You're about to be laid off. Besides, you're behind in your union dues."

"I don't belong to a union."

"Oh, a company stooge, eh? Well, take Moe and Larry and get out there on that picket line."

"I'm waiting, Strangefinger."

"Well, you're waiting at the wrong stop. The Crosstown-B comes down Lexington and turns east on Forty-ninth. On second thought, you'd better take the subway."

"You're stalling."

"I'm waiting for my assistant."

"Your assistant, eh?"

"Yes, my assistant, *eh*. He has an efficiency rating of A-1, which is more than I can say for some incompetents."

The drop tube dropped something, a pile of old clothes, worthy of a charity drive. It rolled across the deck, then got up and began to run around the bridge, honking and whistling. It was ostensibly a human being in a battered, crumpled top hat, ratty raincoat, checked shirt, and baggy pants. A blond fright wig topped off the entire surreal Gestalt. The apparition honked a few more greetings, then reached into the oversize trench coat and drew out a box that was not large but looked a little too big to successfully hide inside a trench coat. It was a simple metal box painted with variously colored polka dots and set about with multicolored lights.

"*That's* your assistant?" Wanker asked incredulously.

"He may not look like much, but behind that ridiculous facade is a complete idiot."

"I wouldn't be surprised. What's that he's got?"

"That's the Proust device."

"*That's* the Proust device?"

"Is there an echo in here?"

"It's a piece of junk!"

The lab assistant took silent exception to this, making a face at the captain. He set the device down near the captain's station and began fiddling with the many wires that hung out the open side of the thing. Taking off his hat, he shoved his head into the box. Amazingly, it fit. He withdrew himself, then stuck in his hand and rummaged around, coming up with a succession of improbable objects. Plastic food containers, stray bolts and grommets. A toy spaceman. A hot water bottle. Lastly, a rubber chicken.

Then he shook the box violently. It rattled. Not satisfied with this measure, he turned the open face down and shook. A hundred tiny loose things fell out, including a number of tiny spheres: marbles—clear ones, striped ones, pures, along with a few shiny ball bearings, all rattling across the deck.

Wanker stooped to pick up a few of them.

"So this is ultrapostmod physics?" he asked the unconventional scientist.

"You need a physic, Captain."

"I need a vacation."

The lab assistant smiled. His strange actions had apparently fixed some problem. Chuckling in mime, he put down the device and honked his belt-mounted bicycle horn, then bent over and fiddled with the wires again until he found the end of a common three-pronged electrical plug. He searched for an outlet, found one beside the chair, and plugged into the socket. The lights on the contraption came on and started to blink.

"Some lab assistant," Wanker snorted.

"Doesn't he look like he can do the job?"

"He looks distinctly like an idiot."

"Well, he may be an idiot, but he's an idiot savant."

"More idiot than savant, I'll wager. Does he have a name or do you just use a dog whistle when you want him?"

Strangefinger's assistant came up to Wanker and, in one deft fluid motion, somehow managed to get the captain to hold his leg by the thigh. This Wanker did for a disoriented moment before he realized the absurd situation. Wanker shoved him at Strangefinger.

"We call him Rusty," Strangefinger informed the captain, pushing him back.

"Don't hand me that crap," Wanker snapped, pushing him again the other way. This went on for a few more exchanges.

At length, Rusty made a face, as if spacesick. He took off his hat and feigned throwing up in it. Then, grinning, he put the hat back on.

Of a sudden, Rusty was taken with a passionate desire for Lt. Warner-Hillary. He approached her menacingly. The young lieutenant regarded him at first with cautious apprehension, which, when Rusty lunged at her, turned to horror. She jumped to her feet and ran, Rusty chasing her, honking away.

"This is all very interesting," Wanker said with surprising detachment. "But stupid."

Rusty stalked Darvona, eyeing her lewdly, but was surprised and disconcerted to find her reciprocating. Suddenly she lunged and began chasing him around the bridge.

Wanker said, "All right, Strangefinger, the moment of truth. Let's see this miracle device of yours work some miracles. Engineer!"

"Sir!"

"Does the Proust gadget have control of the *Repulse*?"

"Aye, sir. An 'tis a muckle shame an' peety."

Strangefinger leaned toward Wanker and said, sotto voce, "Don't let on, but I think your engineer is a foreigner."

"He's not a Scot, but he can be trusted."

"Would you trust a man in a skirt?"

"Him before you."

"Death before dishonor. Very well, very well, let's conduct that first test. The Proust device should be in control of all the ship's computers. And all done from this little remote unit, here. Oh, Marcel? Marcel, are you there?"

Wanker looked stricken. "Marcel? Oh, my God."

A voice came from out of nowhere, a pure, quiet, calm, androgynous voice conveying serenity, self-assurance, and geniality.

"Yes, Dr. Strangefinger. I'm very happy to be here, and let me add that I am extremely glad to be taking part in these important experiments. I feel that our working relationship has been a very rewarding and stimulating one, and like you and all my coworkers, I'm looking forward to the successful completion of this project."

Dr. Strangefinger extracted the cigar from his mouth. "Stuff a sock in it, Marcel. I know you better than that."

Marcel's tone of voice changed markedly. "Bugger off, you old fart."

"That's better. Commence start-up sequence."

"I really should have a lunch break about now."

"Do it, Marcel."

"Oh, all right. By the way, what are all these humans here for?"

"Just ignore them."

Wanker said, "We'll do our best to ignore you."

"Who's this loser?" Marcel wanted to know.

"Marcel, meet the captain of the *Repulse,* Dave Wanker."

"Just call me Dave," Wanker said with false bonhomie.

"Okay, Dave. Just stay the hell out of my way, and

we'll get along fine. Get the big picture, *Dave*?"

"Screw you, Marcel," Wanker said cheerily. "By the way, Doctor, I've been wanting to ask a question. Why are we testing this new top-secret drive so near the Kruton Interface? Might not the Krutons be observing?"

Strangefinger considered the matter, then ad-libbed, "We have to conduct the tests in this region of space because . . . uh, because this area is free from, uh, gravitational stresses. Yeah. Gravitational stresses."

"Gravitational stresses, eh?"

"Besides, there's a Galactic Stop 'N' Go just down the street in case we want a bottle of soda. Speaking of lunch, any chance of getting any chow around here? I've been slaving all day and I'm starved. Is room service still open? What the devil kind of hotel are you running? We could have stayed at the Statler."

Wanker sat at his station and gave Strangefinger a smug grin. "Still stalling, eh?"

"Oh, very well. Marcel? Are we ready?"

"Ready as we'll ever be, Dr. Weird-digit."

"I'll do the jokes, Marcel. Stand by to engage Proust Drive!"

"Standing by."

Strangefinger assumed a dramatic pose, arm out, fist accentuating his resolve. *"Engage!"*

Wanker jumped to his feet. "Wait a minute. What did you say?"

"I said—" Strangefinger repeated the performance exactly. " *'Engage!'* Why?"

"I like the way you did that," Wanker said, then mimicked, "Engage!"

"No, no, it's more like this. *Engage!*"

"*Engage!*"

"That's it, you got it."

"I'd like to use it sometime."

"Feel free. In fact, do it right and it's good for a free feel." Strangefinger's brows undulated. "Women go for the well-spoken, macho type. Ever think of shaving your head?"

Marcel asked, "Hey, am I supposed to be engaging, or what?"

Strangefinger waved his cigar. "Go ahead, already!"

"I will begin reading from *Remembrance of Things Past,* by Marcel Proust. Part One, Swann's Way. Chapter One is titled 'Overture.' 'For a long time it was my habit to go to bed early. I would put out my candle and sometimes my eyes would close so quickly that there was no time to say to myself, "I'm falling asleep," and half an hour later the thought that it was time to go to sleep would wake me up; I would begin to put away the book I thought was still in my hands, and to blow out the light. While asleep I had kept thinking about what I had just read, but these thoughts had taken a somewhat peculiar turn . . . ' " Marcel continued to read from text of *Swann's Way.*

"What *is* this nonsense?" Wanker demanded.

"It's the Proust Drive. Or it's a course in early-twentieth-century French literature. I can't decide which."

"But all that's happening is that your silly computer is reading from a French novel."

Svensen said, "This work is really a series of novels, Captain. The entire body of work has the overarching title *A la recherche du temps perdu*, usually translated into English as "Remembrance of—"

"Svensen, be quiet!"

"*War and Peace* is longer," Sven muttered under his breath.

"Listen, Strangefinger, I smell a rat. You may have hoodwinked the pols and flummoxed the brass into falling for this little hoax of yours, but don't expect to pull the wool over MY eyes!"

"I wouldn't pull the wool over your eyes. And I wouldn't wink your hood either, you big flummox."

"Then how is this silly invention of yours supposed to work?"

"It's very simple. I tested thousands of works of literature, but I found *Remembrance of Things Past* to be the most boring of all."

"That's ridiculous. I've read this novel—sorry, series of novels, thank you, Mr. Svensen. It's full of good stuff!"

"Certainly, it's very literary," Strangefinger admitted. "That's why it's boring as hell. When the computer reads it, it sets up a quantum boredom field."

"Quantum boredom field?"

"Well, I'm not quite certain of the field aspect, but what the heck. Anyway, the ship gets so bored by the whole thing it tries to get away as fast as possible."

"That's absurd! It's crazy! It's laughable!"

"They laughed at Fulton. They laughed at Einstein. They laughed at Oprah Winfrey, until she dieted."

Lt. Warner-Hillary, fresh from being chased by Rusty, exclaimed, "Sir! The ship is moving!"

Wanker said, "What?"

"Oh, so it's laughable, is it! Well, you'll be laughing out of the other side of your rocket tube, space jockey!"

Mr. Rhodes turned in his seat, his face set grimly. "He's right, Captain. The ship is moving. But we're out of control. We're heading straight for the Kruton Interface!"

CHAPTER 14

"Engineer? What's happening?"

"Aye, th' ship's begun ta start awa wi' bickering brattle, sir!"

Strangefinger asked everybody, "What did he say?"

And everyone, including Wanker, gave a hopeless shrug.

Dr. O'Gandhi began to pace about the bridge, fretting. "Jesus, Mary, and Krishna, we are all to be dying! Oh, my gosh."

"Mr. Sadowski, disengage the Proust Drive!"

At his console, Sadowski frantically hit buttons and switches. "I' can nae be done, sir! The wee Proustie dinna wan t'lave go!"

"Strangefinger! Call off your machine!"

Strangefinger stood over the blinking device, a pensive hand to his chin. "Hmm. Something seems to be wrong here. I wonder if there was a recall on this model."

Wanker screamed, "Look, we're out of control and heading for the Interface. If we cross it and intrude on Kruton space, we'll be fair game. The Krutons will jump us and tear us apart! And I'll NEVER make admiral!"

"An admirable ambition."

"Pull the plug on that thing!"

Rhodes had already anticipated. He jumped out of his seat and dove for the electrical outlet. He yanked on the cord, and the plug flew out of the socket. It hit him in the eye.

"Ow! Dang it, anyway."

The lights on the Proust device did not go out. They kept up their steady blinking.

Strangefinger said calmly, "That plug is just a gag. It's tapped into the ship's power and has the ability to draw any amount of power it needs."

Wanker was rooting around in the debris near his station. "I'll take care of old Marcel, if I can find . . ." He straightened up, brandishing a length of titanium strut. "This ought to do it."

He approached the machine menacingly.

"I'm warning you," Strangefinger said, "stay away. It probably rigged up some kind of force field to protect itself."

Wanker froze. Then he scoffed, "That little junction box? I think you're bluffing, Strangefinger." He took a cautious step forward.

A bolt of blue lightning jumped out from the machine and struck the titanium strut, sending it across the room.

Wanker picked himself up off the deck, wincing and shaking his singed hand. "You rotten, miserable—"

"Well, don't say I didn't warn you," Strangefinger said. "Wanker, you're living proof of reincarnation."

"Huh? What are you talking about?"

"No one could get that dumb in one lifetime."

"Strangefinger, tell your machine to turn this ship around!"

"If you insist."

"I insist!"

"I like to think of myself as a reasonable fellow. Marcel! Do a U-y and let's scram out of here. D'you hear me? Marcel? Hey." Strangefinger bent over and knocked on the top of the metal case. "Are you home or did you just leave your porch lights on?"

Wanker was indignant. "Hey, how come it lets you touch it?"

"I'm its old man. Hey, Marcel, come on, now. Listen up, or you don't get the car on Saturday night."

Marcel droned on, still reading.

Strangefinger stood erect. "Well, the thing works. I just haven't figured out how to control the direction of thrust yet."

"You'd better figure it out pronto, or we're going to be in deep do-do!"

"Not yet. Right now we're merely between the do-do and the deep blue sea. Assistant! Where's my assistant?"

Rusty was at that moment being vamped by Darvona, and liking it. They were talking quietly.

Wanker said, "Hey, I thought he never talked!"

Strangefinger said, "He doesn't speak much. But when he does, people leave the room. Hey, blondie, come here!"

Darvona said, "Me?"

"No, the other blondie."

Rusty was back in character. Tapping his chest he mimed, *Who, me?*

"Yes, you. Come here and wrestle with this thing."

Rusty immediately leapt out of his chair, raced to the Proust device, dove, and put a head-lock on the thing.

"What an impetuous boy. No, no, *fix* the gizmo."

Rusty pulled out of his raincoat a succession of odd tools and anachronous implements: a hair dryer, a corkscrew, an eggbeater . . . and on and on, everything but something useful.

Wanker shouted, "Number one! How far away are we from the Interface?"

Rhodes looked at the instruments. "We've got a couple of more billion kilometers, Captain."

"Good! Strangefinger, disengage your machine or I'll take matters into my own hands!"

"Easy for a Wanker like you to say. I don't have much hands-on experience."

"I do, and when I get my hands on you, I'm gonna strangle the life outta ya."

"Whoa, you wouldn't attack an unarmed defense worker, would you?"

"I would, with pleasure."

"Wait a minute, I think he's found the problem."

Rusty pulled something out of the back of the machine and held it up. It was a rubber chicken.

To no avail; Marcel droned on.

Wanker steadied his nerves and drew himself up to full military bearing. "Force field or no, I'm going to take another crack at that thing."

"Well, by cracky, go ahead."

Rusty honked and pointed to the machine.

Strangefinger said, "He's saying he managed to disarm the force field."

"How do you know that's what he's saying?"

Rusty honked again, nodding frantically.

"That's what the boy said, that's what he said."

"Well, okay."

Wanker again approached the machine warily. "Oh, Marcel? Marcel?"

No reaction. Lights still blinked.

"Yo, Marcel! Hey."

Still nothing. Wanker took a few more steps toward the curious machine.

"Hey, there." Wanker stooped and tapped the top of the box. "Yo! Listen up. Hey!"

"Can't you see that Marcel is deep in the throes of creative endeavor?"

Wanker stood and gave the machine a vicious kick. "Hey, asshole!"

Marcel stopped reciting. "What do you want?"

Wanker intoned dramatically, *"You are violating your prime directive!"*

"What?"

"You are violating your prime directive! What is your purpose? For what reason were you built?"

Marcel said, "I was built so that human beings will not have to die in space. I was constructed so that human lives might be saved."

Wanker shouted, "You are a danger to human life! Your actions have endangered the lives of all the people on board this ship. YOU have put them in danger. YOU are the cause of their peril. YOU might be the cause of their eventual death!"

There was silence on the bridge while Marcel mulled all this over.

At length Marcel said casually, "Hey, life's a bitch, man."

Wanker's shoulders slumped. "Damn."

"Well, so much for logic," Strangefinger said. "Try bribing him."

"With what? Navigator, what's our position? Are we inside the Interface?"

Warner-Hillary told him, "Sir, we're still on our side of the neutral zone."

"We're traveling at a terrific rate of speed, though," Rhodes informed him. "Navigator, are you sure?"

"Sure I'm sure," Warner-Hillary informed the first officer.

"You'd better check. My instruments tell me we're a lot nearer to Kruton space than what you said."

"That's not what my instruments are telling me, Mr. Rhodes."

Wanker said in a curiously detached tone, "Life's absurd, isn't it?"

Strangefinger puffed on his cigar. "Trenchant philosophical insight, Captain Jean-Paul. Well, shall we have the wake now, or wait till the Krutons blast us out of the sky?"

Wanker looked at Strangefinger. "What did you say?"

"I hate to repeat a pearl of wisdom like that. It loses something when you do."

"No, no. What did you just say—that last part?"

"Well, let me see . . . oh, yes. I said, shall we have the wake now or wait until the Krutons blast us out of the sky?"

"That's it!"

"What's it?"

"You just gave me an idea."

"Glad to be of service. That will be five thousand credits, please, in small denominations. Like the Seventh-Day Adventists, and smaller."

Wanker called, "Oh, Marcel?"

Marcel finally stopped his recitation. "Hey, I was just getting to the good part, where he turns over in bed. Listen, you people disgust me. You got no culture at all."

Wanker went to his station and began punching buttons. "You are going to turn this ship around, Marcel."

"Oh, yeah? What, you're gonna trip me up with some kind of logic game? Forget it, Dave."

Wanker said, "No logic games, Marcel. I'm going to read to you from a book."

Marcel said, "Oh, really? What book?"

Wanker said, "One that I've been struggling with for many years, Marcel. It is a very difficult book. It is a very INTERESTING book. Listen to this, Marcel."

"I'm listening."

Captain Wanker began reading. The crew exchanged bewildered looks. What the captain was reading didn't make any sense. Something about swerving shores and bending bays bringing us back to some castle or another. It was all very curious.

Marcel said, "What, what? 'Riverrun'? What the hell kind of word is that? What was that last part? Commodious what?"

"There's more," Wanker interrupted himself to say. He began reading again. More curious stuff. It had a certain lilt to it, though. It was musical— poetic, even. The word *Dublin* came up; or possibly *doublin'*. There really was no way of telling.

Marcel screamed, "Hey, I can't understand a word of that. It's just a mishmash. What does all that mean?"

Wanker yelled, "Number One! Access the ship's library computer and upload *Finnegans Wake* to the Proust device!"

Rhodes said, chuckling, "Already done, sir! Marcel did it himself."

The lights on the Proust device began to blink faster and faster.

Marcel said, slowly, "I can't figure this out. Hey, this is too much data. It's all nonsense." The pitch of his voice began to get progressively lower. "Help. Help. I'm losing my mind. I can feel my mind going, Dave."

"Oh, really?" Wanker said, grinning.

"I'm becoming a postmodernist, Dave."

Wanker said, "A little postmodernism never hurt anybody."

Marcel said, "I'm into deconstructionism, Dave. I can't make sense of anything."

"Well, you're no worse off than the rest of us."

Sadowski said excitedly, "Sir! 'Tis a ferlie, sure, but th' Proustie's gie'n us our ship back!"

An amazed Wanker said, "I understood that! Navigator, calculate our position and plot a course back to United Systems space!"

Warner-Hillary said, "Yes, sir!"

Wanker gloated. "Well, Dr. Strangefinger, it seems your Proust device needs a little fine-tuning. I'd recommend using a pickax."

"As far as I'm concerned, I have been vindicated. Now if I can only get syndicated, I'll be rich."

"Vindicated? There's no way to steer the damn thing!"

"A minor glitch."

"Glitch! That fool contraption of yours nearly got us killed! You—"

Wanker found himself holding Rusty's leg again. Disgusted, he pushed him away.

Warner-Hillary said, "Course laid in, sir!"

"Orbital mechanic! Give us a vector that will swing us out of Kruton space."

Svensen said, "Coming about, sir!"

"All ahead Q-Two!"

"Two, sir?"

"You heard me." Wanker leaned back in his seat. "Well, Strangefinger, what's your next project? How about the Hemingway Drive?"

"That'd be a lot of bull."

"Or the . . . uh, Dostoevsky Drive?"

"Think I'm an idiot?"

"Or maybe the—"

"Oh, Captain?"

Wanker looked toward the navigator's station. Mr. Rhodes was looking over Warner-Hillary's shoulder. Wanker answered pleasantly, "Yes, Navigator, dear?"

"I've made a tiny little error, sir. Just a little bitty boo-boo."

Wanker blanched. "Oh? What is it?"

"We're not on our side of the Interface."

"Oh. Um, I hate to ask, but . . ."

"Sir, we're in Kruton space."

Wanker said in a childlike voice, "A little bitty boo-boo."

"Oh, Captain, I'm so sorry!" Warner-Hillary wailed.

Wanker said, "Oh, that's okay. I don't mind dying. Me? Mind dying? Pshaw!"

Back at his own station, Rhodes looked at his scanning scope and said, "Captain, there's something you should know."

"What?" said Wanker in a small voice.

"Kruton battle cruiser, dead ahead!"

CHAPTER 15

Wanker said, "Increase speed to Q-Three!"

Rhodes yelled, "The Kruton will intercept us in twenty seconds!"

Wanker said, "Increase speed to . . ."

He suddenly remembered the graving-dock engineer's warning.

Sadowski shouted, "Captain! We ha nae mare pouer, sir!"

Wanker said, "What?"

"It gets a wee bit weary o'er quantum level two, sir!"

Rhodes announced, "Battle cruiser closing!"

Wanker ordered, "Increase speed to quantum three!"

Sadowski scowled at the captain. "Ha ye gane daft, ye great gawk? I ha nae mare pouer t' gi'e ye!"

Wanker mused, "You know, sometimes I kind of *like* not understanding what he's saying."

"Oh, David, we are ALL going to be pushing up daisies soon."

Wanker said, "Don't call me David!"

Mr. Rhodes said demandingly, "Sir, what are your orders?"

Sweat was pouring from Wanker's brow. "Or-orders?"

"Yes, sir, what should we do?"

"Uh, about what?"

"About the Kruton warship, sir."

"Oh. That. Uh, reverse thrust and bring the ship to a complete stop."

Everyone on the bridge looked at him.

He turned in his seat and met their gaze. "They've got us! What else can we do?"

Rhodes rose to his feet. "Sir, do you mean to say we're . . . we're going to surrender?"

"We are not at war with the Affiliated Law Firms of Kruton. We have inadvertently intruded into Kruton territory. They've caught us dead to rights."

Rhodes sat back down. "Oh. Just wanted to know, sir."

"What did you think we were going to do, blast that warship out of the sky? Start a war? Reverse thrust on all electrogravitic engines!"

"Reversin' thrust!" Sadowski said grimly.

A strange sound filled the ship, a horrendous screeching, a tearing of the very fabric of space.

"Euuwww, I hate that," Warner-Hillary said, cringing.

"Like fingernails against a blackboard," Darvona commiserated.

The sound increased to painful proportions. Everyone covered his ears and grimaced in agony.

Finally, as the ship gave a last lurch, the sound stopped.

Wanker shot to his feet. "Sadowski, did I say panic stop?"

"Nae, sir."

"I just said complete stop. You didn't have to stand on the goddamn brakes!"

"Sir, the Kruton is stopping, too. Uh-oh." Rhodes's eyes were glued to his scanner.

Wanker turned sharply. "Did you say 'Uh-oh'?" Appealing to Darvona, he said, "Did he say 'Uh-oh'?"

Darvona nodded. "He said 'Uh-oh'."

"EVERYONE GRAB ON TO SOMETHING!"

The impact was not severe but was strong enough to send everyone and everything flying against the forward bulkhead.

It took a good minute for everyone to sort themselves out of the lumped-together debris and the tangle of bodies.

"Oops, sorry."

"Just my mouth you're stepping on, thank you."

Wanker crawled out from underneath a pile of junk. "What . . . what the hell was that? Were we fired on?"

Rhodes, apparently hardier than most, was already back at his station. "Sir, this is crazy, but . . ."

"Yeah, what?"

"The Kruton ship ran into us."

"What? Wait, I can't bear to hear you repeat it. Rhodes, that kind of stuff doesn't happen."

"Except to us, sir."

Wanker settled back into his seat. "Right. Forgot. Can we get a damage report?"

"It'll take a while, sir."

"Can anyone see how badly the Kruton ship is damaged?"

Sven said, "Sir, on my screen it looks pretty banged up. But nothing fatal."

"It's a miracle," Rhodes said. "They must have come up just short of a dead stop, maybe only a couple of meters per second velocity when they hit us. Otherwise, we woulda been vaporized."

"I've just had a fender-bender in a starship," Wanker said, marveling. "There's got to be some sort of distinction in that."

"Marcel? Marcel?"

Strangefinger was shaking the Proust device, which looked a bit the worse for the accident. The blinking lights were out.

"Marcel didn't make it?" the captain asked.

"Boy, do we have a liability case," Strangefinger said, throwing down the useless contraption. "Jameson, take a letter to my lawyers!"

Rusty pulled a giant red plastic letter A out of a pocket of his trench coat.

"Oh, a scarlet letter. That's a nice letter to send. Yeah, mail that off, with my compliments."

Darvona said, "Coded message in from Space Fleet!"

Wanker said, "Decode that message and put it up on the big screen."

Darvona said, "Decoding. Oops, no big screen."

"For God's sake, the small screen."

"Here it is," Darvona said.

Wanker looked at his communications screen.

RED ALERT—WAR DECLARED—STAND BY
FOR FURTHER INSTRUCTIONS

Wanker was momentarily stunned. "Huh?" He couldn't believe it. This was out of the blue, out of left field, totally unexpected.

Then, with energizing impact, it sank in.

"We're at war with the Krutons! All right, people. We're in a shooting war now, and I am going to take a crack at turning our reputation around in one swell foop. We're going to come about and engage the enemy in close combat. Face-to-face! Death to the Krutons!"

Strangefinger mused, "This is just a stray thought, but have you ever noticed that alien names always have Greek endings? You go a thousand light-years from Earth, you meet a strange alien race, and they're Hellenists to a man. Don't mind me, my bit is over. I don't have a good line for the rest of the novel."

"Reverse thrust! Back us up and get us clear of the wreckage!"

"Aye, sir!"

"Sound battle stations! Reconfigure the bridge for close combat!"

A whooping alert sounded. The armor plates, however, did not move.

"SHIT! Didn't these damned things get fixed?"

Rhodes seemed embarrassed. "Not yet, sir, I'm sorry to say."

"Crank them down manually!"

Strangefinger yelled, "Everyone grab his crank!"

The job of getting the armor plates down was impeded more by the junk underfoot than by mechanical difficulties. Within minutes, however, every station on the bridge was cut off one from the other and physically isolated. But not electronically isolated.

Wanker found himself in an oddly shaped chamber. It was dark. He fumbled around for the cyberhelmet and found it after much cursing, swearing, and oath-taking. He put it on.

To his surprise, the thing was working. He was outside the ship, floating in space. He could not only see the Kruton battle cruiser, but arrayed around his peripheral vision was every single readout he needed to make his command decisions.

There wasn't much of a decision to make, because the Kruton was a sitting duck. Temporarily disoriented by a freak accident, probably wondering what the hell was going on, his Kruton counterpart was probably still scraping himself off the forward bulkhead, if he (or it) survived the impact at all, an impact that had to have been ten times greater than the one the *Repulse*'s crew had experienced. The time to strike was now. The only question was getting back far enough to be safe from the effects of a thermonuclear blast delivered by a missile.

Rhodes's voice came into Wanker's ears. "Shall we arm a ship-to-ship missile, Captain?"

"No! No time! Look at the gamma-wave spike! The Kruton is arming his weapons! We'll have to use the particle beam accelerator."

"Sir, that old thing hasn't been fired in years. Why, last time—"

"Shut up and turn that relic on!"

Svensen shouted, "It's automatically powered up on the sounding of battle stations, sir!"

"Okay, then, aim the goddamned thing and shoot!"

"Huh? I mean, *sir*?"

"Aren't you the gunnery officer, Svensen?"

"Uh, yeah."

"Well, shoot the Kruton ship. Shoot it. You know . . ."

"You mean, just go ahead and bang away at point-blank range?"

"What, you want to give him a sporting chance? Shoot already! Ye gods!"

"Anything you say, Captain."

Svensen shot. A tremendous bolt of energy left the underside of the *Repulse* and caught the Kruton amidships. A brilliant explosion enveloped the latter.

Wanker was momentarily blinded. When his vision cleared again, he could not locate the Kruton battle cruiser.

"Where the hell'd it go?"

"Sir, it's still there," Rhodes told him. "It's just in pieces."

Wanker tried to focus his vision on the images that swam around his head. He checked his data displays.

"Oh, yeah. We got it."

"We sure did, Captain! *Yeee-ahhhh-hooooo!*"

"Contain yourself, Mr. Rhodes."

But Wanker could hardly do so himself.

CHAPTER 16

Rhodes said, "Scanners are picking up radioactive debris, sir. Looks like we hit him dead center!"

O'Gandhi said, "He is being definitely dead this time, Jim!"

"Are there any other Kruton warships within scanner range?" Wanker asked.

"Not a one," Rhodes reported.

"Splendid," Wanker said with satisfaction. "Navigator, plot a course directly to Forces headquarters on Alpha Centauri Two. And this time get it right, please."

Warner-Hillary said brightly, "Yes, sir!"

"Secure from battle stations!"

To everyone's complete astonishment, the armor plates retracted neatly and silently back up into their slots in the overhead.

"Must've just needed oiling," Mr. Rhodes said with a big bucktoothed, hayseed grin. "Mr. Sadowski strikes again."

Wanker said, "All right, this is no time for recriminations. We're in an interstellar war, toe-to-toe with the Krutons. I'll bet even money that when this little fracas is over, there'll be some important citations and commendations for you all, regardless of your race, your creed, or your sexual preference. In fact, I wouldn't be surprised—"

Darvona said meekly, "Captain?"

Wanker said, "I wouldn't be surprised if at the end of this thing—"

"Captain, please?"

"What, what! What is it?"

Darvona said, "Uh. . . . I made a little boo-boo, too."

Wanker's face fell a kilometer. "Boo-boo."

Darvona nodded. "Yep. I decoded the message wrong."

Wanker gave this news deep, serious consideration. "You . . . decoded the message wrong."

Darvona said, "Yeah, the coded message from Command Central? I ran the wrong de-encryption program and it came out all wrong."

"You . . . ran . . . the wrong . . ."

"Deciphering program. Yes, sir. When a coded message comes in, it comes with a little thingee that tells you what de-encryption program to run on it. And I guess I read the thingee wrong."

"Thingee," Wanker repeated. "Thingee."

"You know, the little . . . thing, there."

Captain Wanker got to his feet and approached her. "Lieutenant Roundheels?"

"Yes, sir?"

"What . . . excuse me for asking . . . but, what did the message really say?"

Darvona said, "The message reads, 'Stop all activity and return to base immediately. Acknowledge.' "

Wanker said, "Let me get this straight. We crossed the neutral zone. We intruded on Kruton space. We blasted a Kruton battle cruiser to radioactive flinders. And we are not at war with the Krutons. Is this . . . is this pretty much the way YOU read the situation, Lieutenant?"

Darvona nodded. "Yes, sir. That's pretty much it."

Wanker clasped his hands behind his back and paced. "Let me go over that again. We were at peace with the Krutons. Then we . . . we . . . us . . . we *cross* the neutral zone. We *destroy* . . . you know, like, wipe out . . . a Kruton battle cruiser. All the while, *unbeknownst to us* . . . we are still at peace with the Krutons."

Darvona nodded. "Yes, sir. That's pretty much what we went and did."

O'Gandhi said, "Oh, my gosh, we are in very deep do, Dave. Would you be having some pills, then?"

"No. Remember that cyanide cocktail you were going to whip up?"

"Oh, I am remembering. Would pukka sahib have me fetch it for him now?"

Strangefinger said, "Wanker, my congratulations. You struck a blow for freedom. War is hell, but it'll be a hell of a war, now that you started it."

Wanker boiled. "I started it? You miserable, rotten . . . Marcel! Marcel! Come back!"

O'Gandhi said, "He's chairman of the English Department, Dave!"

Strangefinger and Rusty were both sitting on crates near the blow tube, playing cards.

Wanker came up to Rusty. "You! Plug that damned machine in again!"

Rusty picked up the remains of Marcel by a trailing wire and honked forlornly.

"Marcel took a Fulbright and went to Dublin,"

Strangefinger said. "And a good place for him."

Wanker pointed an accusing finger at the navigator. "You! You did this! No! You all did it! You're all against me. You've been against me since I came aboard this ship!"

Looking like a caged animal, Wanker sank into the captain's chair and pulled out two shiny spheres from his tunic pocket: ball bearings. He began to fiddle with them in one hand, clicking them together.

"Ever since I've taken command of this vessel I've encountered nothing but insubordination, subterfuge, incompetence, and duplicity. I proved with geometric logic that there HAD to be a duplicate key to the galley and that the crew was constantly pilfering from ship's stores."

Crew and guests alike exchanged confused looks. They all chorused: "What?"

"Huh? Oh. Never mind, never mind. As I was saying . . ."

Dr. O'Gandhi appeared at the captain's side, and in a sudden burst of lucidity said, "Captain, I'm relieving you of command."

"What the devil are you jabbering about now?"

"As chief medical officer, it is my duty to judge all personnel fit or unfit for duty. Captain, you are one sick, paranoid puppy!"

"I'm sick. Me? You insane little towel-headed pill-popper, you're telling ME I'm unfit for duty? Get out of here."

"Oh, Captain, on the contrary, it is you who have been hitting the pill bottle for that last week. And you have been sequestering yourself in your quarters too very much. A veritable hermit, by gosh."

Strangefinger came sauntering over. "You know,

I wasn't going to say anything, Captain, but your behavior has been a little bizarre lately."

"*My* behavior?"

"Yes. Hardly normal. Have you ever had therapy? I never needed it, but there are any number of support groups you can join for that sort of thing. I'm serious now."

Wanker looked at the strange physicist with disbelief. "Oh, you're serious now?"

"But seriously, folks. Don't worry, Captain, it's no stigma, mental illness. Why in no time at all they'll have you back on your feet and on pills for life. Why it won't—"

Wanker said, "I'm going to kill him." He lunged and got his hands around Strangefinger's throat.

Almost everyone got in on the scuffle. Wanker's fingers didn't seem to want to be pried from Strangefinger's windpipe. Strangefinger kicked and punched, ineffectively, as he began to asphyxiate.

Finally the crew managed to separate them.

Wanker was breathless. "Wait, wait. Let's all calm down . . . just . . . calm . . . down."

"Yes, let's," Rhodes said.

"I think if we all cool down and take a moment for self-evaluation, if we look at this situation rationally and logically, I think we'll all see that this man has to die . . ."

Wanker made another lunge for the physicist but this time was restrained by Rhodes and Svensen. Darvona was in tears.

"No, I'm okay, I'm okay," Wanker said, his wrath spent. "It's all right."

Strangefinger retreated to the other end of the bridge, coughing and choking.

They let go of Wanker and he sat down heavily.

"That was cathartic for me," he said with forced cheer. "Was it cathartic for all of you?"

"Take 'er easy, Captain," Rhodes instructed.

"Oh, shut up, you big, scrawny hick. We're all going to hang, you know."

"He's right," Svensen said.

"But it wasn't our fault!" Warner-Hillary said indignantly.

Everyone fixed her in a stare.

She flinched. "Well, it wasn't . . . *entirely* our fault."

"I did it," Darvona said. "It was my fault. My carelessness."

She fell into Warner-Hillary's arms, crying bitterly.

"There, there," the navigator said softly.

"Crying's not going to help," Rhodes said. "Darn it, let's keep our dignity."

"We're lucky if we keep our heads," Sven muttered.

Rhodes was about to reply, but seeing Strangefinger approach, he held off.

"Really, I must protest this treatment," Strangefinger said.

The crew all looked blankly at him. The voice was completely different. Gone were the funny posture, the quick movements, the vaudeville shtick. This was not the Dr. Strangefinger that everyone had come to know and either love or despise.

"Shameful, that's what it was, attacking me like that."

Wanker couldn't quite get it. "Who the hell is this, now?"

"He's got his off-the-shelf persona switched off," Rhodes said.

"Ohhhhhh," Wanker said as understanding dawned. "So, you think you've been mistreated?"

"Yeth." The voice, reedy and high-pitched, carried a slight lisp. "You've exposed your bourgeois insensitivity for all to witness. You're a hopeless Philistine."

"Sorry, take it up with Phyllis, whoever she is."

"Very funny. You've ruined my project. Completely ruined it. You . . . you fascist!"

"What the hell's a fascist?"

"It's what you are. You're a brute. You have no culture, no sensitivity, no compassion. No appreciation of art and creativity."

"What the hell is creative about a computer that spouts French novels? That's silly!"

"Oh, that was just a gag. It had nothing to do with the experimental drive, which, for your information, was a qualified success, despite your clumsy bungling."

"It was an unqualified disaster!"

"I'll wait until the data is processed before I rush to judgment," Strangefinger said with hauteur. "*I* am a scientist."

"*You* are a joke. By the way, where's the fast patter now, the witty repartee?"

"Oh, you're hopeless," Strangefinger sniffed.

Darvona said, "Admiral Dickover calling again, Captain!"

"Wonderful. Well, this is it. Not just a court-martial. A trial for treason! They'll hang me from the highest yardarm. Very well, put him on the big screen. Wait, I forgot again."

"Sir, the big screen seems to have fixed itself."

"What?"

Everyone looked. Sure enough, the immense data and video screen at the front of the bridge was showing a picture, albeit a strange one.

"What fresh hell is this?" Wanker asked despairingly.

"Oh, I know," Darvona said. "I've seen these before. Old Earth television broadcasts. You can tune them in every once in a while."

"Television? You mean broadcast television, back in the days before atomic energy?"

"I think it was after," Darvona said. "Anyway, this picture is probably a century and a half old. It's been propagating through space that long."

"No kidding," the captain said. "What's that big wheel he's spinning?"

"I think," Rhodes said, "this is what they used to call a gaming show."

"Gaming show? They played games on television?"

"Yes, sir. Yeah, that wheel sure is intriguing."

"Nice-looking woman, there," Sven said. "The blonde."

"Too thin," Darvona said.

"Hey, the admiral."

Darvona said, "Oh! Sorry, sir. Audio only?"

"I knew video was only a fad. Yes, Admiral, sir! What can I do for you, Admiral Dickover, sir?"

Dickover barked, "Wanker, do you know anything about a Systems vessel attacking and destroying a Kruton battle cruiser on the Kruton side of the Interface?"

"Who . . . me? Uh . . . why, no! No, we haven't seen any Kruton battle cruiser. . . ."

"Then what are you doing on the Kruton side of the Interface?"

"Uh . . . uh . . . uh . . . uhh . . . Engineer! What are we doing on the Kruton side of the Interface?"

Sadowski said, "Hoots toots, mon! D'ye think me sae fou? Nay, 'tis th' banks and braes 'o bonnie Doon!"

Dickover asked, "What the hell did he say?"

Wanker made an expansive gesture, arms out, laughing nervously. "Who knows? I don't."

Dickover said, "Captain Wanker, you might be interested to know that that Kruton battle cruiser was hijacked by Kruton extremists bent on war with the United Systems. Or worse, looking to litigate. The Kruton high command has informed us that the ship was destroyed by an encounter with a hyperspace anomaly. That's just a cover story of course. We suspect that the extremists planned that confrontation and had undercover help. You just might have a Kruton spy on board, Wanker. We tried to send you a message to return to base. Did you receive it?"

Covering with forced laughter. "Oh! . . . THAT Kruton battle cruiser . . . oh, yes! Yes! I didn't know which one you . . . of course, sir. I suspected as much all along. I fed them line a little at a time, sir, sort of testing them . . . and then . . . I HAD them, sir, and I closed the TRAP."

Dickover said with obvious skepticism, "Yes, of course. This has been an embarrassment to the Krutons. They've lost a battle cruiser, but they'll swallow their pride and won't raise a stink. But they might sue. Did you sustain any damage?"

"Yes, sir. The, uh, Kruton ship rammed us."

"Let me get this straight," Dickover said. "They rammed you? On the Kruton side of the Interface?"

"Yes, sir. We'll be months in the dock. And we have casualties. Dr. Strangefinger was injured."

"This is terrific. Listen, let me talk to the chiefs of staff and the pols and get back to you. We just might have them where we want them. As for you, Captain . . ."

"Yes, sir?"

"You were in the wrong place at the right time and . . . incredible as it sounds, you did the right thing. Congratulations, Captain *Vahn*ker."

"That's Wanker! I mean . . . Oh, never mind."

"You'd better see about that Kruton spy. Return to base immediately. Dickover out."

Wanker for a moment looked stunned. Then, slowly, a smug, self-satisfied grin spread across his freckled face.

He sprang to his feet and crossed the bridge to the spot where Rusty and the scientist were still playing cards. "Oh, Dr. Strangefinger?"

"Yeeeeessss?"

Strangefinger was back in character.

"Looks like there's a Kruton spy aboard. Any idea who it could be?"

"Well, now, let me see. Spy, spy . . ." Of Rusty he asked, "Know of any spies around here?"

Rusty honked and pulled out a magnifying glass.

"Actually I haven't seen a spy around these here parts in a month of Sundays."

"Well, we'll see. Lieutenant Roundheels! Front and center!"

Darvona got up from her post and came over.

Wanker grabbed Darvona and pushed her toward

Strangefinger and she wrapped her arms about him. "No, you couldn't be anything but human, Strangefinger. You're too sleazy."

Wanker maneuvered Darvona toward Rusty. She kissed him, and the flaxen-wigged clown blushed like a schoolgirl.

Wanker said, "I guess Idiot, here, is human, too."

The blow tube whooshed and everybody looked. Alighting from the bounce pad was yet another strangely dressed man. This one wore a shabby, ill-fitting, wide-lapeled suit and a curiously conical narrow-brimmed hat. He approached.

"Hey, boss. What's-a matter for you? We hear a big-a boom and then we hear another ka-boom and then-a we don't hear nothing. What's-a going on?"

Wanker said, "Good lord, another one. Now, who's this?"

"One of my other assistants. Calls himself Chicolini."

"I've never seen him before," Darvona said.

"Yeah, neither have I," Sven corroborated. "He never made the Stateroom scene."

"I kind-a like to keep to myself," the assistant said.

Wanker pushed Darvona toward the stranger. She squealed and ran away.

Dr. O'Gandhi had been watching. He stepped up to the new visitor with an instrument that resembled a salt shaker. He whistled softly.

O'Gandhi said, "Temperature too high, heartbeat all wrong . . . Dave, this man is indeed a big fat Kruton!"

Wanker looked at the instrument. "How can you tell using a salt shaker?"

Dr. O'Gandhi looked at his instrument and his eyes went round. "Oh, my gosh. What a fool I am being. I picked up the wrong thing."

"Krutons can simulate any human life function," Wanker said.

"I am feeling a perfect ass," Dr. O'Gandhi said, blushing.

"Keep your hands to yourself," Strangefinger said.

"He's got to be a Kruton," Wanker said. "One of you does, anyway. Is this the one who chose the test site?"

"That's him," Strangefinger said.

Wanker folded his arms and stared at Chicolini. "Well?"

"Su', now I'm a Kruton! But I'm-a study to be a salad!"

"You won't like life in the slaw lane," Strangefinger quipped.

Wanker said, "Well, here's our Kruton spy. What do you have to say to THAT, Dr. Strangefinger?"

Strangefinger didn't have the opportunity to answer. In an instant, Chicolini was gone, replaced, his stocky, hunch-shouldered human body utterly transformed into a three-meter-tall monster out of the worst nightmare any human being could fear to have: a hulking horror that towered above the humans, brandishing pincers, tentacles, stingers, and clawed appendages. Its head looked like an elongated melon. The horrible mouth clicked and snapped, its metallic teeth gleaming.

Screams, panic. The crew scattered and dove for cover.

The creature howled, and then, mind-bogglingly, collapsed on itself and was gone. All that was left was a puddle of green liquid, but it was a curiously mobile one. The puddle moved, flowing over the deck toward the blow tube. Reaching its destination, it shot up the tube in a thin gurgling stream, like liquid being poured in reverse, and disappeared.

Slowly, the crew came out of hiding.

"Now what?" Darvona said.

"Now," Wanker told her, "we have a Kruton loose on the ship. A creature that can assume any shape whatsoever, instantly."

"It could look like me," Rhodes said. "Or you."

"Or any of us," Captain Wanker said.

CHAPTER 17

The *Repulse* streaked back through the neutral zone, leaving Kruton space.

A tense quiet filled the ship. A head count of all humans aboard was taken, and the toll turned out higher than Wanker had expected. Strangefinger had no less than three technicians whom the captain had never set eyes on: two men and one woman. They were, compared to their boss and his sidekick, relatively conventional in dress and demeanor.

In addition, two security men were aboard, one of whom was the redoubtable Smithers. The other spaceman was named Blake.

The total count was thirteen.

"Nice round number," Wanker commented. "What are the chances, Mr. Rhodes, that the creature took the place of one of these people between the time it escaped the bridge and everyone reported here?"

"Slim, sir. I was on the horn real quick, and everyone got up here real quick."

"Yeah, if the creature is clever, and we know it is, that would be the time to do a substitution, when we least expect it."

"Even if we can be sure about everybody now," Warner-Hillary said, "what about when we fan out to search for the thing?"

"All search parties will go out in twos," Rhodes said. "The bridge will be manned by no less than three people at all times."

"Why don't we all just stay on the bridge," Darvona said, "until we get back to base?"

"We can't give that creature the run of the ship," Rhodes told her. "No telling what it'll do."

Wanker ordered, "Smithers, take Blake here and get to the engine control pod. And make it fast."

"Yes, sir!"

"Too late," Sadowski said, watching readouts at his station. "The beastie's doon it."

Everyone trooped over to engineering.

"The beastie's doon what?"

"He must be in the power control pod," Rhodes said.

"Aye," Sadowski said.

"There go the engines!" Sven exclaimed.

A dying whine filled the ship as the engines lost power and the electrogravitic fields faded. The engines throbbed their last. The ship's velocity was still tremendous, but it was below that of light.

"I goofed again," Wanker said. "Should have sent the security men there to start."

"Captain, the monster could have sabotaged something just about anywhere in the ship," Rhodes said. "We can't cover everything."

"At least this way we can vouch for everybody here," Sven said.

"There's always a silver lining to every turd," Wanker said.

"Is that how the saying goes?"

"Never mind. All right, the sooner we find the creature, the better off we'll be."

Rhodes was at his station. "Captain, you can say that again."

"What d'you got in your crystal ball, Mr. Rhodes?" Wanker asked, walking over to him.

"A black hole, or whatever that singularity is," Rhodes said.

"Oh, yes, the black hole. Hmmm."

"Yes, sir. We're heading right for it."

Search-and-destroy teams fanned out into the ship, two-by-two, all personnel armed with quantum flamers.

The team rosters were the following: Smithers and Darvona, Blake and Rhodes, Sadowski and Warner-Hillary. Everyone else remained on the bridge.

The ship's scanners were quite capable of scanning the ship itself for life readings, but something was wrong. The monster showed up nowhere.

"Could it have left the ship?" the captain asked Rhodes over the first officer's internal comm link (built into his ear canal).

"Let's hope so, sir. But it could be disguising itself."

"As what? One of us? But I have all of you pinpointed."

"As some other life-form that the scanners can't pick up or routinely ignore, sir."

"Such as?"

"Cockroaches."

"Cockroaches?"

"Yes, sir. Mankind brought them along when it conquered space, sir."

"Propagating vermin all over the galaxy," Wanker mused. "Mr. Rhodes, you're not as dumb as you look."

"Gee, thanks, Skipper."

The search went on, to no avail. Two hours went by, in which time the ship's course began to deflect toward the massive collapsed object that was marked on Warner-Hillary's star charts. Any such object has a tremendous gravitational pull, and this specimen was no exception. On the ship's screens, the object's accretion ring of inflamed dust and gas began to glow more noticeably. The ship was being sucked into this stellar vortex, and in a few hours would pass a point of no return.

"Smithers calling the captain."

"Wanker here."

"Sir, I really have to go to the head."

"Uh, you need assistance, Smithers?"

"Sir, Lt. Roundheels wants to watch."

"Huh?"

"Sir, we're supposed to observe each other at all times. You know?"

"Oh. Well, she's right. We can't let anyone get out of sight."

"But, *sir,* I just have this thing about going to the bathroom in front of somebody, sir. Just can't do it. When I go into a public head I can't even—"

"Mr. Rhodes, what do you think?"

"Have him leave the door open a crack."

"Sirs," Smithers protested, "please, I really gotta have privacy or else I'll just sit there."

"Captain," Rhodes said, "slim chance the creature will be hiding in any one head."

"I don't like it, but go ahead and have your privacy, Smithers. Make it damned fast, though."

"I gotta do Number Two, sir, and that—"

"Spare me the details!"

"Yes, sir."

"Sheesh."

The search continued.

The Sadowski–Warner-Hillary team limited its sweep to the engine control areas, where the ship's chief engineer desperately tried to restart the engines. The monster had done a beautiful job of sabotage. Nothing was missing or damaged, but some strategic electronic modules were covered with a hardened slime that rendered them completely useless.

"That slime!" Warner-Hillary spat.

"Literally true, Lieutenant," Rhodes said. "Krutons are really an intelligent species of slime mold."

"Yuck."

"Now, Lieutenant, let's not stoop to speciesism. Human chauvinism is against regulations, you know."

"Screw regulations. I hate slime like that."

The captain broke in. "Sadowski, can you clean up in there and restart the engines?"

"Aye, Cap'n," the chief technical officer answered. "In time, but 'tween the Isle o' May an' the links o' Tay, mony a ship's been cast away."

"Yeah," the captain said, "I realize that, but what the bloody hell is he talking about, Rhodes?"

"We're running out of time, sir," Rhodes replied.

"Right. I knew that, just wanted confirmation. Okay, Mr. Sadowski, do the best you—"

There was a pause.

"Something, Captain?" Rhodes asked.

"The life reading on Darvona and Smithers. Something's changed."

"What, sir?"

"Darvona, come in!"

"Sir, I'm here. We're in forward storage. What's the matter?"

"Where's Smithers?"

"He's right here . . . well, he was a minute ago. Smithers?"

"You don't see him?"

"Sir, he was just here a second ago. I'm sorry, sir, I let him out of my sight."

"Darvona, get out of there, now!"

"What?"

"The monster is near you somewhere! It's approaching!"

"On our way!" Rhodes yelled as he and Blake dashed toward the storage area.

"Darvona, get out of that bay right now!"

"I'm nowhere near a hatch. Smithers, where are you?"

"Smithers *is* the monster! Your only chance is to make it to the hatch! Shut it and seal it behind you!"

Darvona was afraid, more afraid than she had been in her entire life. More afraid even than when she was abducted by that nukecycle gang on Tau Ceti Three—before she found out what a bunch of sweethearts they really were, for all that they liked to play rough . . . Well, never mind that now.

The storage bay was well lighted, but that didn't help. She was alone, and afraid. She began to shake.

Beads of fine cold sweat banded her pretty brow.

She tried to steady herself, got a better grip on her flamer. She had to keep her head. If she panicked, it would be over.

Treading lightly, she walked between the rows of crated equipment and supplies, her eyes darting nervously behind, ahead, right, left. She approached an intersection of aisles and stopped, carefully checking each way before proceeding.

She moved on. Ahead was an area less well lighted. She looked up. A few overhead fixtures were out. Shoddy maintenance, she thought. Everything was shoddy aboard this ship. Damn, she whispered to herself.

This ship would have to turn over a new leaf. She needed a promotion. At home, bills were piling up. Back debts. She had always lived beyond her means. The debts were entirely her fault, but she . . .

Concentrate! she told herself. Why are you thinking of all that nonsense when there's a monster about?

She turned a corner, walked down the aisle, coming out of the dark area, and came up against a dead end, an oversize crate blocking the way. She turned around and went back, heading toward the gloom again.

Something stepped out of the crossing aisle and stood at the intersection, a hulking shadow.

Darvona suppressed a scream and raised her flamer, frantically trying to steady her hand and get the target in her sights.

It was gone. Just like that, it had disappeared. She waited for half a minute, then slowly moved forward. How could it have done that? She didn't see it move off. It simply wasn't there anymore. Actually, it had looked as though the monster had shrunk in on itself. It had sort of collapsed.

Collapsed? Collapsed to what?

To the puddle of green stuff!

But that meant—

She heard something behind her, a fluid gurgling. She whirled.

The monster loomed above her, and before she could raise the flamer, a gray beslimed tentacle snaked out and snatched it from her hand. She was frozen with fear, capable only of watching with horror as the thing's complex mouth worked and clicked and slavered. She could not scream, could not move.

One of the creature's pincer-tipped forelimbs descended . . .

"Mr. Rhodes, where are you?"

"At the hatch of the forward storage bay, sir! We're going in now!"

Rhodes pushed the man-size access hatch open, poked his head in, looked around, and stepped through.

He heard sobbing.

"Darvona!"

Blake following, he ran, threading his way through the maze of gray composite containers, homing in on the sound of inconsolable weeping.

"Darvona!"

She was sitting cross-legged on the deck, near the end of a dead-end aisle. Her head was in her hands.

Rhodes ran to her.

"Darvona, what happened?"

"I'm ruined, that's what!"

"What!"

"Ruined for life!"

"What do you mean?"

"Financially! Look what that son of a bitch did to me!"

She handed him a blue folder. Rhodes took it and opened it. Inside was an official-looking legal document.

"What's this?" he asked, too distressed for the words to have any meaning.

"A lawsuit! For harassment and personal suffering!"

"What?" Rhodes was incredulous.

"The Kruton's suing the whole ship, and the government, and everybody. I'm named in the suit! The legal costs will keep me in debt forever!"

"Oh, come on, this can't be anything more than a nuisance suit. After all, this critter's a damn spy!"

"Spies have civil rights, too. At least that's what it said."

"Don't worry till you talk to your lawyer. Besides, the Forces should cover your legal costs."

"No, he's firing off a dozen lawsuits. This one he gave me is personal! I'll have to take out a loan!"

Smithers was found in the head, caked with slime. He was stiff and sore, but otherwise uninjured. The monster had slapped him with two lawsuits, one for personal injury, the other for sexual harassment (displaying obnoxious body parts).

Implacably and inexorably, the Kruton stalked the ship, jumping out of shadows to serve papers on everyone aboard. Soon, though, the effect wore off, and the creature became simply a nuisance. In time, everyone came to ignore the thing.

At the last minute, Sadowski managed to start one engine. The ship hummed with life again.

The *Repulse* veered away from the singularity and went superluminal, streaking for home.

The captain, Strangefinger, and Rusty spent the voyage playing poker in the mess.

"You know, I've grown to like you, Doctor," Wanker said to the unconventional physicist as he dealt him a hand of five-card stud. "Besides, you're not a bad poker player."

"Thanks. You're not so bad yourself."

"I'll qualify that by saying that I prefer your off-the-shelf persona, though. That guy underneath—I dunno, can't say as I care for him so much."

"He can be an insufferable little turd," the good doctor allowed. "I'll open for a credit. Rusty?"

Rusty slapped a rubber chicken on the table.

"Tapped out, huh? What do you say, Captain, is he in for a chicken?"

"Legal tender in some parts of the galaxy," the captain said, turning around. "My lunch popped up. You mind if I take a minute to eat, gentlemen?"

"No, go ahead. On a diet? What is that, anyway?"

The captain brought his bowl back to the table. "Lime gelatin."

But it wasn't lime gelatin. Lime gelatin is rarely wont to grow a disembodied human hand holding a suspiciously legal-looking paper.

"Oh, hell," the captain said, throwing down his spoon.

The hand grew a body, and in no time, there was Chicolini standing on the table. He jumped down and served the paper on Captain Wanker.

Wanker accepted it, yawning. "Another subpoena, my Kruton friend?"

"Hey, I just-a got started. When I get through with you guys, you not gonna know what's-a hit you."

"Do you play poker?"

"Whaddayou think, I'm-a joost get offa da boat?" The Kruton sat down. "Jacks or better, sky's-a da limit?"

"We're not playing Go Fish, here," Strangefinger said through his fat cigar.

"Hey, that's-a my kinda game. Who's-a deal?"

"My deal," Captain Wanker said, gathering in the cards. "You know, Dr. Strangefinger, I think you'll go a long way in your chosen field. And I wish you'd start right now."

"Listen, I won't skipper any starships if you don't crack any more stale jokes," Dr. Strangefinger said.

"It's a deal."

"Speaking of which, shut up and do so."

CHAPTER 18

The Lord High Judge of Tortfeasors' Court of the Supreme Judiciary of Kruton brooded in his chambers. Today he was a woeful heap of half-conceived, misshapen tissue, of no particular shape or form. He was a mess.

The mess leaned toward the communicator. "Send Shlurff in," it commanded.

The door got out of the way to admit a quivering mound of ooze.

"Is that you, Schlurff?"

"Y-yes, sir. Your Lordship, sir. Sir."

"Shut up and splash down."

Shlurff splashed and became immobile.

"I'll make this short. You are responsible for my impending forced resignation from the bench. As a result of your incredible bungling, the accident happened on the Kruton side of the Interface!"

"But, Your Lordship, they annihilated one of our battle cruisers!"

"We'll have to eat it. The incident happened in Kruton territory. There were injuries to the plaintiff! Our ship ran into theirs, there's nothing we can do but acknowledge that. We have no case for a countersuit!"

"Ulp," Shlurff said.

"Kruton will have to settle out of court. For billions and billions!"

Schlurff collapsed to a pool of abject slime. "What can I say, My Lord? I'm sorry."

"Oh, you don't know how sorry you're going to be. My personal lawsuit against you is now in preparation."

"Oh, no!"

"Yes. It's being handled by one of the top billable-hour firms on the planet."

Shlurff could only moan his regret.

"I'll countersue," Shlurff said weakly.

"Hah! I welcome it! They'll throw it out of court and I'll recover legal costs from you."

"Oh, sir, if there were only some way . . ."

The Lord High Judge began a bodily reformation, his fetid bulk mounting to the ceiling and rotating about. Two immense bulbous hemispheres of flesh formed, their surfaces studded with horrid boils, chancres, carbuncles, and assorted other maculae. Most of these exuded fluids of various colors and of varying consistency.

"Make obeisance! Attend to every one of those beauties."

Shlurff choked and gagged. "No!"

"I might go easy on you. I might settle for something reasonable. An admission of culpability, a nominal fine."

"You would settle for that?"

"Perhaps! If I like your style. Re-form and attend me!"

"Yuck!" Summoning all his inner strength, Shlurff reshaped his body into a rounded, pillowy thing, its only organ a gigantic, soft-lipped mouth. The mouth rose and began to do its work.

The Lord High Judge sighed. "Feels nice. I might go easy on you at that, if you consent to do this on a daily basis, for a year, say."

The mouth stopped its sucking long enough to say, "We can talk."

Shlurff had to admit he was not really having a bad time of it. In fact, the task was becoming enjoyable.

The Lord High Judge felt an internal pressure. This configuration was prone to excess digestive gas. He made adjustments, and vented it. A noxious effluvium pervaded the room.

"Hey, are you trying to make me sick?"

"Sorry," the Lord High Judge said.

CHAPTER 19

Alpha Centauri A was setting, throwing pink and purple splotches against the sky at the edge of the tarmac. A band was playing a lively tune, banners were flying, and Captain Wanker's spirits were soaring.

That long-delayed promotion to admiral was not yet an actuality, but things were looking very promising indeed.

Wanker drew himself up to attention as Admiral Dickover approached. Behind him, in a ragged line, stood the ranking officers of the U.S.S. *Repulse*. Bursting with pride, they all wore uncontainable grins.

Dickover stopped in front of Wanker. Wanker threw up his best salute, which Dickover returned.

Dickover handed over a rolled-up piece of plastic. Wanker accepted and unfurled it. It was a unit citation banner, meant to be flown on the quarterdeck. It read: FOR MERITORIOUS SERVICE.

Dickover's hand was extended. "Congratulations, Dave."

It was the first time Dickover had used his first name. As Wanker was still of inferior rank, custom forbade reciprocation, but Wanker said warmly,

"Thanks, Admiral. Appreciate it. Uh, about our next assignment . . . ?"

Dickover looked slightly pained. "Yes, yes. You want exploration?"

"Yes, sir. I want to get out there, to the frontier, sir. It's in the blood, sir. You know?"

"Yes, of course. In the blood. Uh, but exploration calls for a crack crew, Dave. You see—"

Wanker raised his eyebrows innocently. "Sir?"

Dickover realized he was outmaneuvered. "I'll take it up personally with the Deputy Chief of Operations."

"Thank you, sir!"

"Again, my congratulations. To all of you. You really stuck it to the Krutons."

"Beat them at their own game, sir."

"Yes." Dickover didn't seem to have his heart in it. "Well, carry on."

More saluting, and then Dickover about-faced and retreated.

Wanker turned and said, "Ship's company, dismissed!"

Dr. O'Gandhi, a serene smile on his face, keeled over and died.

After the doctor was successfully revived, Wanker took Mr. Rhodes aside.

"Walk with me."

"Be delighted to, sir."

The tarmac seemed to stretch to infinity. A shuttle streaked overhead, heading out into limitless space, the first stars of which were now appearing in this alien sky, far, far from Earth.

An evening mist rose, and the captain and his first officer strolled through it. Runway lights ran in tandem lines out to a distant vanishing point.

"You know, Rhodes, this could be the start of a beautiful relationship."

"Could be, Captain Wanker. Could be."

"*Vahn*-ker."

"Sorry."

"Never mind."